AF441756

MY WHOLE WORLD

JOKER'S SIN BOOK ONE

DAVIDSON KING

My Whole World

Joker's Sin Book One

Copyright © 2020 Davidson King

https://www.davidsonking.com

ALL RIGHTS RESERVED

Cover design by: Designs By Morningstar

Editing done by: Flat Earth Editing

Proofreading provided by: Flat Earth Editing and Anita Ford

Interior Design and Formatting provided by: Flawless Touch Formatting

The unauthorized reproduction or distribution of this copyrighted work is illegal. No part of this book may be reproduced or transmitted in any form or by any means, including electronic or mechanical means, including photocopying, recording, or by any information storage and retrieval systems, without express written permission from the author, Davidson King. The only exception is in the case of brief quotations embodied in reviews.

This book is a work of fiction. While references may be made to actual places and events, the names, characters, places, and incidents either are products of the author's imagination or are used fictitiously. Any resemblance to actual persons, living or dead, events, or locales is entirely coincidental.

Licensed material is being used for illustrative purposes only and any person depicted in the licensed material is a model.

Trademark

No part of this publication may be reproduced, stored in a retrieval system, or transmitted, in any form or in any means – by electronic, mechanical, photocopying, recording or otherwise – without prior written permission, except in the case of the brief quotations embodied in the critical reviews and certain other noncommercial uses permitted by copyright law. Please purchase only authorized electronic or print editions and do not participate in or encourage the electronic piracy of copyrighted material. Your support of the author's rights is appreciated. This book is a work of fiction. Names, characters, places, and incidents are a product of the author's imagination or are used fictitiously. Any resemblance to actual events, locales, or persons, living or dead, is coincidental. All products and/or brand names mentioned are registered trademarks of their respective holders/companies.

WARNINGS

Violence. Not suggested for people under 18.

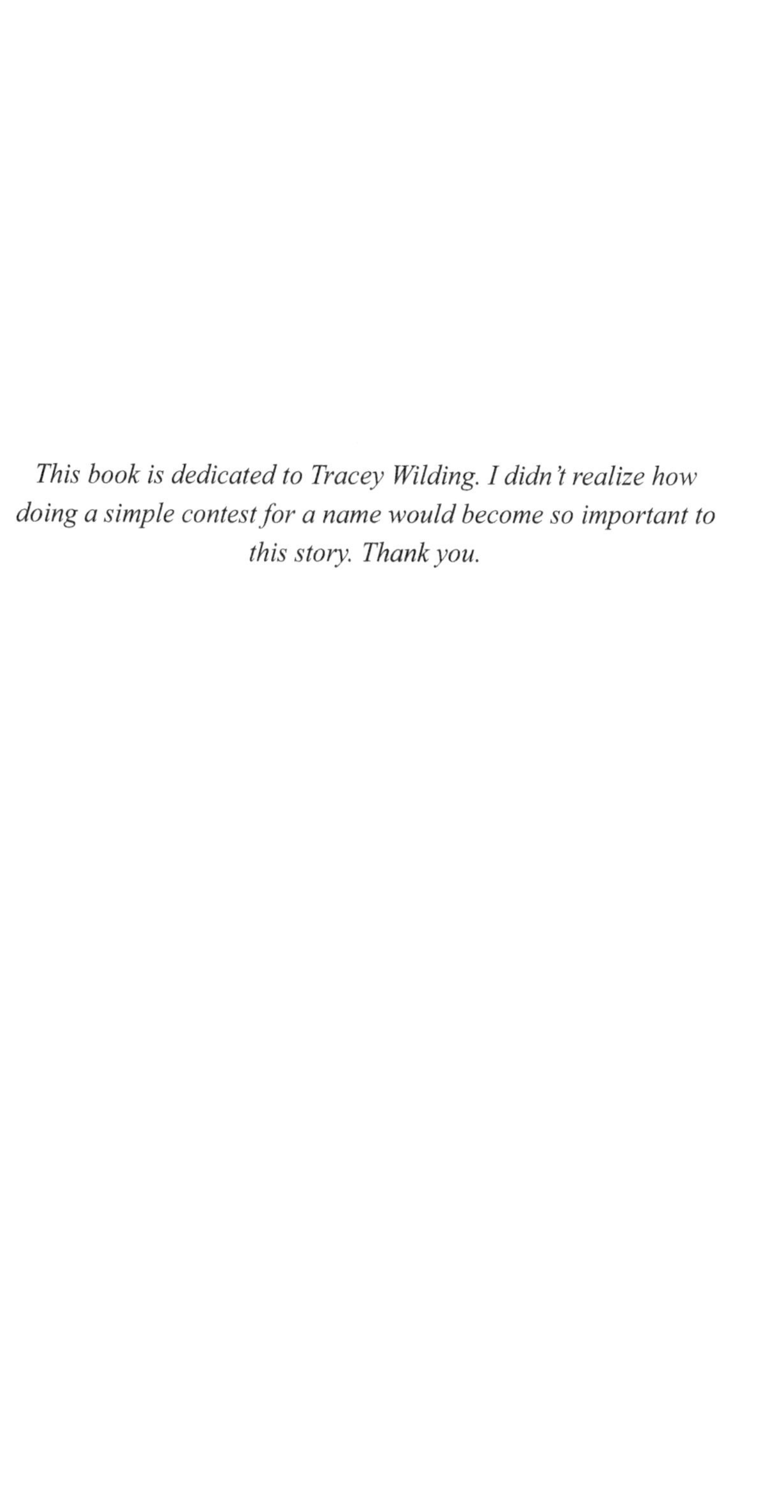

This book is dedicated to Tracey Wilding. I didn't realize how doing a simple contest for a name would become so important to this story. Thank you.

CHAPTER ONE

Atlas

All my life, I wanted to have purpose. Growing up in foster care will make you seek out something to belong to, and when I couldn't fit in, I created my own home. A world built around me…and I employed it with a bunch of misfits. Joker's Sin was the type of place I'd dreamed of. It fed my need to entertain, and everything was played by my rules. It had a rocky start, and sure, I made some shitty business decisions at first. But now, it was the most popular gay bar and nightclub in Haven Hart. Through the many years I'd been here, I'd seen other clubs come and go, and gay or not gay, none held a candle to Joker's Sin. The only one around for the last two years was Vick's Tricks, and what an eyesore that place was.

Joker's Sin was unique, with spontaneous themed days only my staff was aware of. If patrons wanted to know what they were walking into that night, they had to check out the Joker's Sin website, and Lord help you if you showed up dressed like a sexy alien on 80s night. My head of security, Ciro, would just make a swipe with his hand, and you'd be gone. I knew what worked and what didn't work in this business, and it was my whole world. If anyone tried to come between me and its success, they'd be met with a very angry man.

"Keith quit." Max, my bar manager, rushed into my office in a panic. "It's Saturday night, Atlas, and I have no floor manager to help it all run smoothly."

Fuck. "What? Did he walk in, quit, and leave?" I shut down my laptop and stood from behind my desk, knuckles pressed against the dark wood. "Max, Keith wouldn't just up and quit."

I loved Max like a brother, but the way he was squirming told me there was a lot more to this story.

"We fought. Is that what you want to hear? He said I was a whore, I called him a prude-ass, he told me to go fuck myself, threw my bar rag in my face, and left." Max pointed to his face, mystified by Keith's reaction.

"And you know he quit, how? Maybe he just left because he was angry."

"Oh…yeah…Ciro confirmed he quit."

I rounded my desk and stood before Max, a good four inches taller and a lot broader than him. I knew I had a threatening stature when the situation called for it. Max was one of my best friends, and I didn't want to scare him, but it wasn't the first time this had happened.

"How'd Ciro know Keith quit?"

"Ciro came over to me after my argument with Keith and said Keith told him to tell you he quit. But I said I'd come tell you, and Ciro hates getting involved in personal drama so…" He lifted a shoulder nonchalantly.

"Max," I growled. "This is the fifth employee in a year that has quit because you couldn't keep it in your pants. I love you, but Keith's right. You're a whore. Fuck another employee, and I'll kick your Italian ass right outta here, friendship be damned." His expression was worrisome, and I was glad to see my words were affecting him. "This is my business, my world, and you're making it difficult when you act more the playboy and less the bar manager I hired you to be. You get one more fucking chance."

"Atlas, come on, I—"

"You're done fucking employees." I raised a brow. "Got it?"

"Fuck. Fine."

"Good. Now, I'll work the floor tonight. Get on the website and post that we're looking for a floor manager with experience. I'm sure we'll get bites real fast." And we would. I was asked daily if there were job openings.

"Yeah." Max's cocky expression was back on his ridiculously handsome face. He was an unsteady guy when it came to love. He fucked until he was tired and then moved on. That was all well and good if the other person involved understood it. Me? I fucked when I needed an itch scratched. Love wasn't for me, and I was never unclear about that fact with any of my lovers.

After Max left, I moved to the room next to my office. It was a dressing room of sorts with a bathroom and shower. Since I performed every night in one way or another, I needed this space. Working the floor was no exception; it was all still a performance. The floor put me into the thick of it, which I didn't mind so much, but I felt centered when I was on my stage. *Ahh, my stage. My pride and joy.*

When I had the club designed, I wanted it to be unique, somewhere no one had ever been to before. The stage, while the focal point, wasn't all Joker's Sin was, but it was where I felt at home. It was a huge circle protected by the bar that ran its circumference. No one could get to the stage unless they jumped over the entire bar, and that wasn't happening. The only way on or off was the back stairs, which always had security—not to mention, my DJ stood on a raised section against the stage wall. When I opened the stage for dancers, personally selected by me or him, that was the show right there. He overlooked everyone, the

Master of Music, and he thrived on it just as much as he hid inside it. He often said he got a serenity from the vibrations, from people transforming with the sounds, and that was something I could relate to. It was his peace and for him to understand.

I chose a purple silk shirt and black leather pants and brought them with me to the bathroom to take a quick shower. When I was managing a station, I dressed one way and then changed when I was on stage. It was how I got into the right headspace for the moment.

I hung my clothes on the back of the door, grabbed a thick and sturdy hair tie, lifted my braids, and wrapped them up. I didn't have time to go through the procedure of washing my hair since I had to be on the floor in an hour, so I'd just wash my body.

Under the spray of the water, I thought about how the night would be altered now that I'd be on the floor.…And wasn't that always a fun game? I loved being kept on my toes in situations like this.

I dressed and sat in front of my large vanity. I wasn't a man who feared makeup or signs of femininity, and I was a showman who liked to look good. I was blessed with amazing genes: my dark skin was always impeccable, my honey-brown eyes practically glowed, and I loved adding a little liner to help them pop even more. My mama didn't give me much, but she did pass along her good looks.

Even though I grew up in foster care, I knew who she was. I remembered her vanilla scent and how she hummed. I also remembered how she tried to sell me for drugs once, and that memory overpowered everything else.

"Hey, Atlas, you coming out?" Max shouted from my office, and I left to meet him.

"Of course I am." I smirked when I noticed how he was drinking me in.

"Damn, if you weren't like a brother to me, I'd fuck you."

Laughing, I pushed him out the door. "Since when would me being your brother stop you?"

"Eew, man, even I have limitations."

I rolled my eyes and followed him out into the fray. *Fuck, I love my life.*

CHAPTER TWO

Toby

"You're looking good, Toby." My sister, Poppy, wheeled herself into my bedroom, fighting her way through the doorway.

"Thanks. It's my only night off so—"

"So you're going to Joker's Sin and hoping super-duper hard that *The Atlas* will see you, save you from your dull and poor life, and whisk you away." She batted her eyes at me comically, so I threw a pair of socks at her, making her giggle.

Poppy was all I had in this shitty world. We were twins in every sense of the word. We looked alike: wavy brown hair and matching eyes, same height, same laugh…same everything. We both even liked men. When we were eighteen, during the summer before college, we went hiking. I was responsible for her. At one point we decided to climb around a steep hill, and I told her I'd go first, keep her safe by tying a rope around her and connecting it to my waist. Every time I remembered that moment, my stomach rolled. In one second, everything changed, everything crumbled. The rope got loose and she fell; I don't think I will ever forget how she screamed. My mistake left her paralyzed. She had to hold off on college until she'd healed, accepted, and adjusted to her new normal, but she'd lost interest by the time the doctor gave her the all-clear. For years the guilt ate at me, until Poppy got angry one day. Told me climbing that hill was as much her choice as it was mine, and she refused to live a life shrouded in guilt. For her, I tried. I would always wish I caught her or did something differently at that moment, and nothing she could say would change that.

My parents did what they could, but our father passed when we were twenty and our mom just a couple of years later. We lost ourselves in the grief of mourning our parents and at the end of that tunnel, we clung to each other. Drew strength from what we had together.

I wanted to provide for her, but I left college after my second year and fucked around so much, that when I was ready to work, all I could get were shitty jobs. Poppy worked for a seamstress and was able to do so from home while I spent my nights mostly at Vick's Tricks, doing whatever Vick asked me to do.

On my nights off, I loved going to Joker's Sin; I wished I were a part of that world instead of the one I was in. Poppy spent these nights with her friends doing what she called "Drunken Book Club." I loved that Poppy had a group of amazing friends and that even though we were the most important people in each other's lives, we had our own to live.

"So what book are you all on now?" I shot her a grin. "And what are you drinking?"

"Oh, Toby! It's a good one. *City of Girls* by Elizabeth Gilbert."

"The *Eat, Pray, Love* author?" I asked as I used my fingers to comb styling gel through my hair.

"Yes, very good, my young padawan. And we're drinking four different types of wine."

"Just remember, if they get drunk, you can't have them in my room."

"*One time*, Toby." She chuckled.

Turning, I folded my arms. "She was drunk, and I didn't know she was there and when I slipped into bed, she kept calling me Mr. Darcy and tried to get me to 'make a baby.' " I used air quotes.

Poppy was laughing so hard, tears danced in her pretty brown eyes. "Classic fun."

I rolled my eyes and moved in front of her, pushing her through my doorway. "I'll be home late. No women in my bed— that's just mean."

"I need to get more guys to come to my book club." She pouted.

"Then I might not mind if they try to make a baby with me in my bed." I winked, snatched up my keys, and left to the sound of Poppy's contagious laughter.

———

"ID." The bouncer outside Joker's Sin was no joke at all. His name was Ciro, and he ran all things security-related. He was huge, head shaved close to the scalp, always in black, and I don't think he ever smiled.

"Oh, shoot. I left it in my other boy shorts." The twink in front of me clearly had never been here before and thought he could bat his glittery eyes and get Ciro to let him in.

"Guess you better go back home and get it, then," Ciro grumbled and waved his hand dismissively. "Move."

The twink was at least smart enough not to argue, and he did move on.

"Hey, Ciro," I said as I offered him my ID.

"Hi, Toby, go on in." Still no smile but he was at least nice to me.

"Thanks."

The doors opened, and as always, the sounds and smells hugged me right to my soul. It was crazy how at home I felt here. Whenever I went into Vick's, I felt dirty, greasy, and like I was in some purgatory. I accepted my life, but it didn't stop me from dreaming of one that was right here in this magical place.

It was clear from the music playing that it was a full-on dance night. I was glad too, because I'd forgotten to check the website to see if there was a theme tonight. My eyes went right to the stage where the DJ was on his pedestal. I loved how there was a song playing and a video to go with it behind him on a huge screen. This one was a remix of "The Spark." I'd be sure to add it to my playlist.

Bodies were jumping, swaying, spinning, and so in tune with the music, it was almost poetic. Each person who entered this place felt that "it." I didn't know what "*it*" was, but it invaded you, and you were honored to be "*its*" slave. If you went there sad and depressed, out of sorts or lonely, it was as if the magic of the place wouldn't let you feel anything but amazing. "*It*" would move your legs, force a smile, make you love just being alive.

I walked over to the bar; Max must've been on the other side, so I ordered a watermelon margarita from another bartender and watched the stage that stood above the bar.

"Here you go, sweetheart." He winked and slid my drink over. It was nice to think I was desired by someone even if he was just doing his job.

"Thanks." I sipped the delicious drink. Fresh watermelon squares made up the ice cubes—so fresh, so different from Vick's.

It was obvious Atlas wasn't on the stage, and for a moment I wondered if maybe he wasn't working tonight. Spinning on the stool, I scanned the crowd on the floor. It was a sea of people, but

I knew he'd stand out. I heard a cacophony of laughter so loud it jolted me, I turned and there he was. The center of attention, surrounded by at least twenty people listening to whatever he was saying. I couldn't make out his story, but the animation on his gorgeous face told me it was probably the best story ever told. Just looking at the man made my heart ache like a lovesick child.

"You got it bad, sugar." I turned around at the voice. I'd seen the guy around sometimes, but he never talked to me. He had hot-pink hair, stunning makeup, and was dressed in some sort of glittery jumpsuit.

"Um…what do you mean?" I shrugged and set my half-empty drink down.

Hot-pink man lifted his chin, gesturing to where Atlas stood. "I don't have time for pretending you don't know who I'm talking about. You got it bad for Atlas."

Rolling my eyes, I didn't deny it. "Yeah, me and like a hundred other people."

He chuckled. "Try more like thousands." He stared at Atlas as if he were a science experiment, and I was intrigued by what would come out of those bright-purple lips. "I don't think I've ever seen him with anyone longer than a night."

"Have you two, um?"

He laughed, transforming his entire face from sharp glamour to stunning joy. "Oh, hell no. Atlas is a hell of a guy, but I don't need that love 'em and leave 'em sort of thing." He held out his hand. "Everyone calls me Sparkles, who are you?"

"Oh. Toby." Shaking his hand I noticed his nails were red glitter and…wow, he was a show in himself. "I love everything about your outfit."

Sparkles smiled. "Thanks, sugar. I'm a work of art, what can I say?"

"You can say you'll let me drive you home tonight." Sparkles and I both turned toward the deep voice. Max stood there with a hungry gaze aimed at Sparkles.

"Aww, aren't you sweet. But if I wanted herpes, I'd just head on over to Vick's."

Sparkles's reaction only made Max huff, but I couldn't hold back my laughter.

"I don't have herpes. Come and…come on." Max gestured to his cock.

"And they say romance is dead," Sparkles said and looked at me. "Don't sleep with *that* ever. You'll likely die of something long and hard to pronounce." With that, Sparkles took the drink Max gave him and sauntered off.

I finished my drink, ordered another margarita, and got lost in whatever Atlas was saying to his admirers. A guy could dream.

CHAPTER THREE

Atlas

"What are you doing tonight?" I tried to remember all the regulars at Joker's Sin, but there was no way to get everyone straight. I didn't recognize the one currently offering himself to me, however.

"Working."

He chuckled and slid his hand over my silk shirt. "Let me rephrase." The guy stood on his tiptoes, and I played along by leaning down to help him out. "Who are you doing later?" he whispered.

"What's your name?" Placing my hand over the one he had pressed against my chest, I made sure to give him my full attention. It took balls to put yourself out there and tell someone you were interested in them. I wasn't about to make him feel less than the brave man he was.

"Lance."

"You're very sexy, Lance." And he was. He had on super tight jeans, a sheer white shirt, and he did his hair and makeup in a way that screamed he gave a shit. "I gotta work till close, though. I'm short a guy, but…" I said when I saw his lips dip. "Gimme your number. I'll call you when I'm done for the night, and if someone else hasn't snatched you up, I'll gladly take you up on that offer."

Lance was fast. He pulled his phone from the back of his too-tight pants and handed it to me. I wasn't an idiot. I never gave my number to one-night stands. I'd take his digits and call from my office when I was done. I learned that the hard way.

"Gimme your digits." I handed him his phone and took my own out. I knew he likely wanted to have my number, but he didn't argue. After I had it, I excused myself to check out the rest of the floor.

Ledger—DJ Edge to everyone here—had just started another song, and when I walked up the stairs and signaled to him that I was going to get ready, he knew he had to prepare. I quickly went into my office and got into my stage wear.

———

"Good evening, one and all!" I loved the roar of the crowd as they focused on me, at center stage. All the dancers had moved to the floor, and it was just me and Ledger. "This crowd has been amazing, haven't they, DJ Edge?"

"Oh, hell yeah, Atlas. The best," he said into the mic attached to his headphones.

"They deserve a reward for being so great." I eyed the crowd that was cheering and shouting how much they agreed with me.

"All of them?" Ledger asked. "You should make it fun."

This was part of the act, and Ledger had it down pat. "Oh, you have an idea?" With my microphone in hand, I moved closer to him. "Tell me."

He hummed, and I knew the echo of his voice was sending shivers through everyone. Ledger was a sexy fucking man and rivaled me in getting attention from the patrons. "I say we pick five people to come up here and dance. The winner gets…" I loved how he paused for dramatic effect and how everyone was eating it up. "…dinner with you."

Oh, how the crowd was loving this. We often did things like this: rewarded them with dinner, a lap dance, or something more with either myself or Ledger, and on occasion, gifts. We hadn't had many bad experiences, and we made sure security was close by.

"Dinner you say, hmm. Wonder where we'll go."

Ledger chuckled, "They get to choose." Even more roars from the crowd now.

"To make it fair though, neither one of us should pick the dancers, wouldn't you say?" Now I was walking closer to where Max was working below. "Max, pick someone you want up here dancing."

He turned, narrowing his eyes at me, hating when I made him part of my show. "Pain in my—" he started to say but stopped when one of the other bartenders shoved a mic in front of him. "I choose Sparkles." Of course he did. He'd wanted to bang that glittering beauty forever and likely thought getting him up here would give him brownie points.

"Okay, Sparkles, where you at?" It didn't take long to spot him. He sat on a barstool, bright-green drink in hand, looking like a rainbow. He was glaring at Max something fierce, and I couldn't help but laugh. Like a good sport, Sparkles hopped off the stool and made his way over to the stairs.

"Heya, Sparkles." I winked and handed him the microphone.

"Well, good evening to you, Atlas." His smile was sinful. "I assume you want me to pick the next dancer?"

"That would be fabulous," I spoke into the mic that was in Sparkles's hand.

"Very well." He walked all along the stage. So many people shouting his name, begging for a chance. He winked, blew kisses, really worked the crowd. He stopped, smiled at me over his shoulder and said, "Toby."

I knew the name, as it wasn't incredibly common. When Sparkles pointed, I followed his finger to a terrified-looking guy. Wavy brown hair with purple highlights, full pink lips, and a "deer in the headlights" expression. No question, he was someone I'd love to spend time getting up close and very personal with.

Walking over to Ledger, I gestured for another mic, and he tossed it into my hand. "You sure, Sparkles? He looks like he doesn't want to be up here."

Toby hadn't moved at all, even with Max telling him to join us. I didn't want him participating if he'd rather not. Oddly, I felt a pang in my chest to get the spotlight off him and make him not look so terrified.

"Oh, trust me, he's just wondering how he got so lucky." Sparkles chuckled. "Come on, Toby, get your cute butt up here and show me how you shake it."

So slowly, slower than I'd ever seen anyone get up on this stage when summoned, Toby made his way over. I watched, intrigued by the shy, adorable guy. I'd heard Max and Ciro mention him, but I'd never had the chance to meet him. Like I said, I always try to remember the regulars. And watching this trembling cutie move closer to the stage did something to me. I'd certainly remember meeting him.

What felt like a year later, Toby stood beside me. He had to crane his head to look me in the eyes, but I found I liked how he stared at me. Twinkling brown eyes, a light shimmer of eyeshadow, and liner decorated his gaze. Stunning.

"Hey there, Toby," I said and brought the mic to his mouth.

"Holy shit," he practically shouted, making the whole place laugh.

"Wow, you got some fire in that body, don't you?" I shared a look with Sparkles that said he was likely out of his depth. "Well, Toby, I'm Atlas."

"Um, yeah, I know…I…you're great." Toby rolled his eyes, and I felt his embarrassment. That wasn't my intention, so I chose to move on.

"How about you pick the next person? If you don't know their name, simply point, sweetheart." I winked and Toby's Adam's apple bobbed, his lids fluttered, and yeah, he was enamored. It was sweet. But I'd be lying if I said I wasn't intrigued by the shy beauty standing before me too.

Sparkles came over and handed Toby his mic and stood beside me. After Toby took it and started walking the stage, stiff as a robot, Sparkles covered my mic with his hand.

"That guy comes here once a week, only has eyes for you. And not in a creepy 'I want to wear your skin' way. Trust me, he's living a fantasy right now."

Nodding, hoping Sparkles was telling the truth, I continued to watch Toby.

"How about that person?" Toby pointed, and I saw he was referring to Lance, because of course, that was my luck. I was okay with that, though. Even if Sparkles was hoping I'd let Toby win, I was totally up for feeling Lance all over too. But as I saw Lance's beaming smile and Toby's hesitant one, I couldn't help wishing I'd met Toby earlier in the night instead of Lance.

"Ahh, Lance." I gestured him onto the stage, and he practically ran.

"Looks like I get more time with you sooner than we planned, huh?" Lance said into the mic, and for some reason I turned to see if Toby had heard, but it was into the microphone, so of course he had. And damned if his frown wasn't equally as adorable as the rest of him.

When we had all five dancers on the stage, I began explaining the rules. "Okay, boys. There are rules." All but Toby groaned. He appeared to really be afraid. "DJ Edge will start the music; you dance the best you can. There'll be a chair." One of my security walked up at that moment with one and placed it in the center. "There will also be streamers." I moved over to Max, who held up two pairs of dancer's streamers, I took them and put them on the chair. "We also have a dancing cage." I pointed to the ceiling, where a cage slowly dropped. "And two, yes two, poles." I took a step back as two dancing poles rose from the floor. "After each song, one of you will be eliminated. When the last one is standing, you'll be deemed the winner."

Sparkles smirked, Lance was clapping, and the other two seemed excited enough, but I was worried about Toby, who was already sweating.

"Okay, let's begin, shall we?" I gave Ledger the cue, and he started the first song.

CHAPTER FOUR

Toby

I couldn't do this. I mean, I wanted Atlas to finally notice me, but not like this. There was a reason I only sat at the bar when I came here. I. Couldn't. Dance. Not like the music intended, anyway.

"Shake it, sister," Sparkles said to me as he took my hand and tried his hardest to get me to move.

"I can't dance."

Sparkles's eyes widened. "But…" He looked around; everyone was watching Sparkles and me *not* dancing. "That's what you do here."

"Move it, boys," DJ Edge's voice rang out. I saw Lance and the others dancing like their lives depended on it. One took to the pole and another to the cage.

"Leave me, save yourself," I urged Sparkles.

"I never leave a man behind." He winked and I watched as he grabbed the chair Lance was about to sit on and dragged it over to me. "Sit."

I did as I was told because I was terrified and everyone was watching, even Atlas. He crouched down over by Max, and they were talking.

"Let's do this, tin man. I'll get you oiled up." And Sparkles straddled my lap. "Grab my ass." I did exactly as I was told; I sat there while Sparkles danced on my lap. He was like liquid as he slid to the floor, climbed up, and wow, he was really rubbing himself on me. "Touch me," he said. When I glided my hands along his waist, over sequins and rhinestones, I felt so alive. The crowd was cheering, and Atlas only had eyes for us.

Through the corner of my eye, I saw one of the other dancers move over toward him, twirling streamers and doing their hardest to get his attention. But he was transfixed, and it made me feel bold. Sparkles stood for the briefest of moments, and I followed. When I gripped his hand and spun him, he gasped. I wasn't the bump-and-grind kind of man, but I remembered how my dad would dance with my mom in the kitchen.

"Are you slow dancing with me?" Sparkles smiled.

"Add some flair and just…yeah, it's all I know."

With a wink, he slid an arm around my waist, and we spun all around the stage, in our own wonderful world. He laughed when I dipped him, and I couldn't hold back my joy. I was having so much fun, I almost didn't realize the music stopped.

"Well, well, that was a twist I didn't see coming." Atlas's laughter boomed through the entire club. "You two, get over here." Sparkles took my hand, and we moved to where Atlas and the other three dancers were. None of them, besides Atlas, appeared too happy with us.

"Where'd you learn to dance like that?" Atlas asked me.

"Oh, um…my folks. My dad loved dancing with my mom in the kitchen…" I heard Lance snicker and saw the other two roll their eyes.

"You did all that by just remembering how your pops and

your mama danced?" When Atlas smiled, it drowned out all the negativity coming from the others.

"Yes."

There was a brief silence before the crowd started whistling and hooting.

"Okay, then." He turned to the other dancers. "You." He pointed to one, I couldn't remember their name. "Thanks for the dance with the streamers, but you didn't make the cut. Max, give the man a free drink."

The man's bright smile faltered and, shoulders slumped, he walked off the stage. "And then there were four," DJ Edge said.

"Indeed. Let's slow things down this time. Sparkles and Toby, do that again. Lance and Chad, you two partner up. Dazzle me with some slow dancing. Best couple remains, and I'll choose from the two of you." Atlas waggled his brows and pointed to the DJ. "Make it happen."

"You got it." DJ Edge did his thing, and a slow song began to play.

Sparkles once again wrapped his arm around my waist. "Show a girl a good time, would ya?" He smirked, and I would do exactly that. I wasn't sexually attracted to Sparkles, though he was gorgeous, but he made me feel relaxed, like myself.

Once again, I tuned out everything but Sparkles and the music, like we were in a cloud of melody and laughter. We danced until the sounds of the crowd burst through, and the song came to an end.

"Damn!" Atlas shouted into the mic. "You two are on fire." He was speaking to us, much to the chagrin of Lance and Chad. "You two are absolutely still in it." He turned to the other two. "Great try, guys. Max, drinks for these two, please." Chad shrugged and walked off, but Lance looked livid. Atlas lifted his brows and stared him down until he stormed off the stage.

"That was amazing, but how do we judge who out of the two

of you is the winner?" He tapped his chin and looked out into the sea of people. "What do you think?" He gestured to someone sitting on a stool.

"Dance with each. Best one wins." The guy seemed very pleased, and I could tell by the grin on Atlas's face, he liked that too.

"Perfect. Who's first?"

"I'll go," Sparkles said, not giving me a chance but at the same time giving me the moment I needed to calm my shaking nerves.

"Let's do this."

Atlas tossed his mic to Max, and DJ Edge began to play something, I wasn't sure what it was, because all I could do was watch as Sparkles and Atlas danced in perfect symmetry. I didn't think I could compete with that. They laughed like lifelong friends. And when the song ended, Sparkles whispered something into Atlas's ear that made the big guy chuckle.

"Thank you for the dance," Atlas said once he got the mic from Max. "Now, Toby, your turn."

I realized Atlas was going to be leading, and I took a deep breath and stepped into him. DJ Edge started the music, and I knew this one. "Fire on Fire" by Sam Smith.

My hand slipped into his, and he placed one of his on my back and crushed me to him. It felt more like flying and a lot less like dancing. He pulled me up, to the point I swear my feet weren't touching ground. The feel of his breath on my neck told me that was exactly what was happening. We weren't dancing together at all; Atlas was taking me on a ride, and I never wanted to get off.

It all felt like a dream, and if I didn't win this contest, if I was never in Atlas's orbit ever again, I'd cling to this moment. When my lungs felt like they were seizing from the stresses of life, I'd remember his scent. When the world was falling all around me, the way he felt pressed against my body would be my happy place. In times of darkness, this moment would save my life.

The song ended and I slowly crept back to earth and wanted to weep when he stepped away. Our eyes met, and I wondered if he felt that dance like I did. *Would it save his life too?*

"You're one hell of a dance partner, Toby." He whispered into the mic, almost like he was in awe of me, but that couldn't be right.

"Thanks, you're um…not too shabby yourself," I said and the mic picked up on it and the room laughed.

"I know when I've been beat." Sparkles winked and sauntered off the stage.

Wait. What?

"Congratulations, Toby. Looks like you and I are going on a date." Atlas gently touched my cheek and I stood there, frozen.

No fucking way. I was going on a date with *The* Atlas Durand?

CHAPTER FIVE

Atlas

I told Toby to talk to DJ Edge, and he'd make sure to arrange the dinner. I was so intrigued by this man. When I pressed his smaller body to mine, it was like something clicked. The perfect dance partner had to not only physically mold to you, they had to be mentally in sync.

Sparkles meshed with me in that carefree, no-strings-attached, this is fun sort of way. Toby was so much more intense, and I felt it in every fiber of my being. His gaze told a million stories, and I had to stop myself from kissing the words out of him.

The rest of the night went on as it always did: People talking and touching me. Numbers being slipped into my back pocket. And quite a few people enquiring about the job Max had put up only a few hours before we opened. By the end of the night, I felt how I always did. Content. It was a successful night, and patrons were happy.

"Hey," I heard Lance's voice as I leaned on the bar, waiting for Max to get me a water.

"Hey, yourself. Good dancing up there tonight." I gestured to the stage.

"Not good enough though, right?" He wasn't angry, but I could read his frustration.

"Just because your tight ass makes me hard doesn't make it a fair enough reason to let you win." I pushed off, grabbed Lance by his belt loops, and turned him so he was now against the bar and I was pressed close to him. "Doesn't mean I'm not going to give you a prize for tonight."

"Oh, God, yes please." He gripped my shirt and moved to kiss me.

"Not here. It's last call. What say you sit right here and when I'm all done, we head out?" He nodded excitedly. Smiling, I took the water that was placed in front of me, chugged it, and moved to close the place down.

———

"KNOCK, KNOCK, KNOCK," Ledger said as I sat at my desk the following afternoon. "Got a sec?"

"Yeah, what's up?"

He sat, wearing a Cheshire grin that would make anyone nervous, but I'd known Ledger a long time. No matter what came out of his mouth, I'd deal.

"Have fun with the third runner-up last night?" He was referring to Lance, and while we'd had an amazing night, I wasn't going into details with Ledger.

"It was sex, Ledger, and since when does curiosity about my sexual partners have you coming into my office, smiling and bothering me?"

He chuckled and ran his fingers through his black hair. "Right. I just wonder if you'll ever *maybe* keep one longer than a night."

"Why? You never do."

He lifted a shoulder nonchalantly. "We're talking about you."

"Then I'm ending the conversation." I turned my attention back to my computer, reading an application for floor manager.

"Fine, new topic. Toby St. Claire."

Hearing Toby's name sent a wonderful tingle right to my balls. "Mmm, yeah, what about him?"

"He chose Vayne's for dinner, but the thing is, the dude only gets one night a week off, so it can't be until next week, Saturday." Ledger scrolled through his phone. "I called Xander Vayne himself, and he said he'd hold a table for seven o'clock and to let him know if that doesn't work."

"Saturday night? Ledger, that's impossible. I need to be here on Saturdays. He can't maybe get another night off during the week?" Me not being here on a Saturday wasn't an option.

Ledger scrunched his face. "Didn't sound like he had any wiggle room with his boss."

"Where's he work?" He shrugged. "Did you get Toby's number?"

"Yeah, want it?"

Nodding, I wrote it down as he said it. "Okay, let me talk to him. I can't imagine any boss making it near impossible to change a day off."

"You got it. I'm going to be going over the song lineup today for next week, you want to see it when I'm done?"

I chuckled. "Do I ever change it?"

"Nah, but you have a theme for Saturday, Women of Rock. Didn't know if you wanted to see what I choose."

I shook my head. I trusted Ledger to do the job I hired him for, and just like I wouldn't let anyone tell me how to do mine, I wasn't about to insult him by telling him how to do his.

" 'Kay, see ya." After he left, I stared at Toby's number for a good minute. What would I say to the guy?

"Fuck it." I picked up my office phone and dialed.

"Hello?" Toby answered, sounding a little unsure, which likely had to do with the number coming up as Private Caller, since he had no idea who was on the other end.

"Toby, hi, it's Atlas Durand." Hearing Toby gasp put a smile on my face. I was used to people being enamored with me but with Toby, I found I enjoyed how much he was affected.

"Hey, um…hi."

"I'm actually calling because Ledger, or DJ Edge as you know him, informed me you could only do the dinner with me on Saturday?"

I heard a voice in the background, and Toby shushed them. "Um, yeah. I work six days a week, and Saturday is my designated night off. Which is probably really cool for some people to have off. But I imagine for you that's not a good day, seeing as you have to work. So, I understand if you need to cancel. Thanks so much for the opportunity though, and—"

"Whoa, whoa, come up for air, Toby. It's okay. I'm not canceling." I was, in fact, going to see if there was any way he could talk to his boss, but he seemed a little high-strung, and I suddenly wanted to hug him and tell him to breathe.

"You're not?" he squeaked, and I couldn't help but chuckle.

"Nah, but I do have to work, so I wanted to run an idea by you."

" 'K, sure."

I didn't have any idea at all, so I had to think fast on my feet. "I love that you chose Vayne's; it's one of my favorite places. And Xander, the owner, is an amazing chef. So, how about I order from there, and you join me in my office for a candlelit dinner here? That way, I can spend the evening with outstanding company and still be available if there's an emergency."

I didn't want Toby to feel like I was squeezing him into my night or life. I did want him to enjoy it, and I was interested in talking with him.

"Oh, wow that's even better. Thank you!"

"Perfect. I'll let Ciro know you'll be here at five, so maybe we can get a little quiet time before the doors open. Would that work?"

"Absolutely. Thank you for all this." I smiled at the sincerity in his tone; it tugged at my heart in a way I wasn't used to. Sure, he might have stars in his eyes, but something told me Toby had his feet firmly planted on the ground.

"My pleasure. I look forward to seeing you Saturday."

After we hung up, I felt better that I didn't cancel or make Toby's life harder. I got lost in the applications and was able to pick three people I was interested in meeting. Max was setting up interviews. Since we all had to work together, I liked to have Max, Ledger, Ciro, and myself in attendance, interviewing as a team. Each of us held a position in Joker's Sin, and together we made the place run smoothly. No way would I bring in someone who could throw a wrench into this well-oiled machine.

CHAPTER SIX

Toby

I had just finished making sure the bar was fully stocked at Vick's Tricks when I heard my boss call my name. Shane, the bartender and a good friend, looked up and rolled his eyes. Working for Vick was like trying to navigate around land mines— you never knew when things were going to go fine or when you'd sneeze wrong, and he'd fly off the handle.

He was also a dangerous man. I'd seen him do things that haunted my dreams. Poppy had told me so many times to just quit, that we'd figure things out. We had a small savings, but I liked to keep it there, unused, in case of emergencies. Poppy didn't make a lot as a seamstress; she covered a couple of bills. My paycheck from Vick's was double hers. I needed this job.

I shut the dishwasher and hit Start. Shane patted me on the back as I made my way toward Vick's office. I knocked, entering when I heard him say to come in.

"Toby, yes, good. Have a seat." He gestured to the rickety-looking chair across from him. Carefully, I sat.

"Is there something wrong, sir?" Nervous bubbles fizzled in my stomach as I waited to hear why I was called into his office.

He chuckled and looked behind himself where Liberio, his main muscle as I called him, stood. "No, you're fine, but…" He wagged a finger. "I found out something very interesting about you."

As quickly as my brain could process, I ran through everything about my life that could, even a little bit, interest Vick.

"What's that, sir?" I could feel a bead of sweat trickle down the side of my face.

"Liberio here went to Joker's Sin on Saturday to scope out the competition. Trying to figure out how exactly we can maybe push them out of the way and be the bigger, better show in town."

If I wasn't silently panicking inside, realizing that Liberio saw me on that stage, I'd be scoffing if Vick thought he could hold a candle to Joker's Sin.

"Ha ha. From the look on your face, you're freaking out." Vick's green, squinty eyes and slicked-back blond hair were a stark difference from Atlas's honey-colored eyes and shiny braids. And I took a moment to remember the dance…to find my happy place.

"I go there sometimes, I um…" My eyes darted to an emotionless Liberio. "I wasn't aware that wasn't allowed."

Vick cackled and slapped his desk. "No, boy, calm yourself." He reached in his desk drawer and pulled out a pack of cigarettes. "Liberio said you got yourself a date with the man himself, Atlas Durand." He put the cigarette in his mouth and lit it.

"Um…yeah."

"Congrats. Good for you." I couldn't tell if he was being genuine or sarcastic, so I gave him a small smile and waited. "You have given me an amazing opportunity."

Him? "I have?"

"I want Vick's Tricks to be something more than it is. This last year, I've lost almost forty-five percent of my clientele because they're over there at the faggy place." He held his hands up. "I know you're gay, Toby, no disrespect." What was I going to do, fight him?

"None taken, sir." I clenched my fists; I knew I couldn't yell at Vick—he'd have me laid out in a second if I tried.

"I was thinking maybe you winning that dance thing could benefit us all."

Fuck my whole life. "How so?"

He blew a stream of smoke from his mouth and smiled. His yellow-tinted teeth and smarmy grin made me want to run out of there and shower.

"See if you can't maybe poke around in Atlas's head. Get some info out of him." He shrugged. "Nothing too intrusive. Just maybe feel him out…literally if you have to."

Was he asking me to sleep with the man to get information on Joker's Sin? I didn't have to vocalize the question; that was exactly what he was saying.

"When do you have this date?"

I scratched behind my neck, a nervous gesture. "He knows I only have Saturday off, so we're doing a dinner at the club in his office."

"Ok, good, that'll work. Sunday, you come in, and we'll talk. It would mean a great deal to me if you had something to tell me. Anything at all that may help me out. No matter how little, but definitely the bigger the better." There was a warning in there; I heard it, and Vick knew I did.

"Yes, sir."

He sat back and waved his hand, causing ash from his cigarette to fall on his pants. "Good, now go." I was happy to get the hell out of there.

When I got back to the kitchen, I was shaking. "Hey." I

jumped when Shane put his hand on my shoulder. "It's ok, just me."

"God, Shane, I hate this place," I whispered.

"Yeah. Not a lot of job opportunities these days, though. I put in two applications last week. Vick called me into his office and reamed me a new one when he found out."

"How'd he know?" Wide-eyed, I watched as Shane paled.

"How's he know anything, Toby? He just does."

It was true. About three weeks into me working here, a cocktail waitress named Franny told us she spent her days off at a strip club, working the pole. Said in that one night, she made more there than a week here and was trying to get extra hours there so she could quit working at Vick's.

The next day I came into work, and she and Vick were yelling something fierce. A day later, Shane and I found out Franny was in the hospital with two broken legs and a concussion. Vick Keller wasn't a man to be trifled with.

"What happened?" Shane asked as he helped me organize the kitchen for when they opened. Vick's wasn't anything like Joker's Sin. We served finger foods, there was a small stage for performers, a bar, pool tables. So different. How Vick thought he could ever make this place into anything close to Joker's Sin was beyond me.

I explained everything to Shane, and when I was done, he let out a low whistle. "Damn, Toby. What're you gonna do?"

"I dunno. I'll maybe see if I can learn anything from Atlas. Something that won't be too big, and hopefully that'll make Vick happy."

Shane offered a small smile. He was a good-looking guy with his bright red hair and gray eyes. I knew he was bisexual, but neither of us had ever shown interest in each other. We clicked as friends and never thought to try for more.

"Good luck, Toby. I'm here if you need to talk." He left after that to finish his tasks before opening, and I took a moment to calm my frantic heart. This place was a pit of despair. Hearing how Vick reacted to Shane simply applying to other places sat heavy on my chest. There was no way I'd get away with secretly applying anywhere.

I worked my shift, and grease, grit, and booze soaked through my skin and clothes. By the time I got home, Poppy was asleep and my legs and feet were killing me. I wanted nothing more than to faceplant on my bed, but there was no way I wanted the scent of Vick's on my bedsheets. So I showered as fast as I could, threw on a pair of boxers, and did exactly what I wanted to do. Sleep.

CHAPTER SEVEN

Atlas

"So, Ethan, tell me about this experience you have here. Says you managed a club in New York called Dive." Ethan was the first one we were interviewing. Joker's Sin didn't open until later, so I was holding the meetings right in the club, on the floor with Max, Ledger, and Ciro in attendance.

"Yes. Oh. My. God. It was the best ever. I mean, this place is the best ever, but yeah, best." He then winked at Max, and it took everything in me to hold in my groan.

"Best ever isn't really an answer," Ledger deadpanned.

"Oh, um, well, okay. So I oversaw the hosts and servers, made sure there weren't issues between the bar and the waitstaff. I saw to it that the right people were on the floor. Things like that." I noticed he kept shifting his eyes toward Max.

"Do you two know each other?" I pointed between them.

"What?" Ethan's voice rose an octave, which told me everything I needed to know.

"Yeah, I'm sorry, Ethan. I don't think this will be a good fit."

"Oh, come on. I didn't know Max was here, I swear." Ethan was arguing, and I found it hard to believe him.

"I'm sorry."

"That's illegal." Ethan stood, hands on his hips. "You can't not hire me because I slept with someone who works here. I would never sleep with him again."

"What the fuck!" Max stood, taking a step toward Ethan. "What about the last time we fucked? You were all, 'Oh, Max, I love your cock, best cock ever.' "

I believed Ethan said *exactly* that, but seeing those two going at it right in front of me didn't bode well for the working environment or chemistry I needed with my staff.

"This is why, Ethan. I can't have this. Have a good day." I nodded to Ciro, who quickly guided an irate Ethan out the door.

"Max, is there anyone you haven't slept with?" Ledger chuckled.

"Yes, your mom."

"Very mature." Ledger scoffed.

"When's the next interview?" I stood, stretching my back and loving the way it cracked and popped.

"Half an hour, then no more for an hour after that." Max gathered the applications. "I don't recognize the name of the next one, so I'm fairly certain their virtue is safe."

For the remainder of the day, until about two hours before we opened, we had interviews but of the many we saw, only two were qualified. And we weren't totally in love with them either. The place was set up for the night, so everyone left to spend the next couple of hours getting ready, eating, whatever they had to do. I opted to spend it in my office with some Chinese takeout, the show *Sex Education*, and thought about what I'd be wearing that night.

———

ON THURSDAY we announced on the website that Saturday was Women of Rock night. I wasn't sure what Ledger would play, but we'd be sure to make it an amazing night. I would be sporting some kickass Joan Jett and the Heartbreakers garb, wearing black kohl around my eyes, and make it a night to remember. I hoped Toby would have no issue with the theme and embrace it when he arrived. I told Ciro he was coming that night around five and made sure to inform Toby in advance what tonight was, so he wouldn't stand out in a bad way after our date if he wanted to stay in the club. Seeing as no one who wasn't wearing the appropriate attire would be admitted, he had to blend in.

I was just putting the finishing touches on the elegant table I had set up in my office when I heard a knock on the door.

"Come in."

Turning, I saw Toby enter. He wore white ripped jeans, Converse sneakers, and a vintage Blondie T-shirt. His make-up was subtle, but his hair had flecks of glitter throughout.

"Oh, wow," I said as I approached him. "I am loving this." I brushed my hand over his shirt, thrilled with the reaction I got when I did.

"And you." He gestured to my outfit. I was wearing my black leather pants and a shirt with Joan Jett's face on it. "Great choice."

His cheeks pinked so beautifully. Nature's blush. "How about we sit?"

Toby nodded and sat when I pulled out his chair. "This looks amazing. Atlas, thanks for making it work with your schedule. My boss wouldn't have let me move it around, so I would've understood if you'd had to cancel."

"Ha. There was no way I was canceling. You won fair and square." I lifted the silver domes over the dishes. I had called Toby earlier in the day and asked him what he'd like. He chose a simple chicken marsala, and I opted for a T-bone steak and baked potato.

"Smells like heaven." I watched as he closed his eyes and took in the aroma of the food. His dark lashes fanned across his cheeks and in that moment, he was blissful to witness.

"Vayne's is one of my favorite places," I said as I poured us each some wine.

"My sister and I have gone a few times. It can be expensive." His eyes widened. "Oh, I didn't even think about that when DJ Edge asked me which place. Here." He started pulling out his wallet.

"Toby, stop." I didn't yell but I made sure to be somewhat forceful. "You won, you chose. I knew that going in. Do not insult me by offering money."

Toby's cheeks pinked once again. "Okay, thank you."

"You're welcome. Now tell me about your sister." I listened as Toby talked about his twin sister and what she did for a living. I noticed that when he mentioned she was in a wheelchair, his voice cracked. I wanted more information as to why, but I didn't know Toby well enough to intrude on that privacy.

"And what about you?" Toby asked. "This place, how'd you decide on the name?"

Of all the questions I thought he'd ask, that surprised me. It was one I never answered and besides Max, Ledger, and Ciro, no one knew the story behind the name. But as Toby sat there with his dark, innocent eyes, having talked for a full twenty minutes about his life, I decided to give him the truth. It was like a pull, like I wanted him to know. And while that should've freaked me out, it didn't.

"It's named after someone I used to love a great deal."

His brows furrowed, no doubt as confused as I'd expected him to be. "Was their name Joker?"

I chuckled. "Nickname, because he was always joking around.

Getting himself into trouble. I always told him one day karma would catch him."

"Did it?" Toby whispered as the thumping of the music from the club began, and I knew Ledger was getting ready to have Ciro open the doors. The sounds were like a pulse, always vibrating through me, giving me life.

"It did."

"And you called him Joker. What was his sin?"

"Making me love him, I guess." I wasn't sure who was shocked more by my admission. I felt like I could go on for hours talking about my life with Toby. He made it feel so easy.

"I'm sorry, Atlas." He reached across the table, his hand brushing over my fingers. "Naming this place Joker's Sin implies you think you're a sin, and I just can't see that. You give so much to the people of Haven Hart."

I gave his fingers a squeeze, then sat back with a chuckle. "I don't think that's true. I give them entertainment."

He shook his head, lips turned down. "I don't think you understand how important letting go and freeing yourself from the binds of life can be. I choose to come here every night I have off because it's my therapy."

I wanted to ask him what he felt bound to, what made him need to break free from everything, but there was a knock on the door, and a second later Max popped in.

"Hey, sorry to interrupt, but there's a commotion outside. Some guy hit Ciro with a bottle, cops are here." Starting the night this way was never good.

"Fuck." I stood so fast, I almost knocked the table over.

"Oh, no. Is Ciro okay?" Toby was righting things, and I knew I had to cut this short.

"Yeah, we were just getting ready to open, and some guy wasn't dressed to theme. It didn't go over well; I think the guy was high."

I was glad I had Toby come before we opened but hated that I had to go out and deal with this. "I have to go talk to the police, Toby, I'm so sorry."

Toby rolled his eyes. "Yes, how dare you make sure your employee is okay, and your place isn't being taken over by drug-induced ragers."

I laughed. "Please stick around for the night. This won't take too long, I hope."

I left my office and quickly made my way out front in time to see a medic applying a Band-Aid to Ciro's forehead. The speed in which the ambulance and authorities arrived surprised me. I really hoped this mess wasn't a sign that it would be a bad night.

CHAPTER EIGHT

Toby

I stayed in Atlas's office for about ten more minutes. I thought about maybe looking around, seeing if I could find something that would appease Vick enough so he wouldn't be upset. I walked over to his desk, but it was immaculate, not a paper in sight. All the drawers appeared to be locked. I didn't dare try to pry any open, because with my luck there were cameras in the room, and Atlas would catch me. I went back to the table and made sure everything was as clean as it could be. Then I slipped out the door.

The club only had maybe twenty people in it. I imagined they were all outside, either waiting to get in or watching the police and medics. When I went over to the door to peer out, I saw the police pushing someone into a cruiser, and I knew who it was. He was a regular at Vick's. When Max said the guy was high, I believed it. And I also knew it was likely Vick that was supplying him. I wondered if Vick had him come here to act this out? But why, when he knew I was trying to get info?

An idea wrapped around me, and I knew I might be able to

make this work. If Vick wasn't satisfied with what I told him—
which I still didn't know what that would be—I could blame the
tweaker and maybe get a pass. I had to hope.

I took a seat at the bar, and one of the bartenders asked me if I
wanted anything, but I just ordered a soda. My eyes scanned the
crowd, and I saw more people begin to trickle in. Either Ciro had
returned to work or Atlas was taking over.

Max and Atlas were still outside, and DJ Edge began playing
some kickass music. Women of Rock was a great theme, and I
was glad it seemed he'd be spotlighting women from all decades.

Out of the corner of my eye, I saw two guys starting to argue.
There was a bouncer there but without Atlas, Max, or whoever
was supposed to be managing the floor, it was too much for the
bouncer to handle. Especially when three others came over. I
listened for a moment to see what was wrong. One guy was upset
because the other stole his drink. Another was blaming the drink
owner for showing up here with his ex. So dramatic. I thought
about what Shane or I would do at Vick's. Liberio would likely
punch one and drag him out, but Shane and I always had our own
ways of handling things.

"Excuse me," I said to the bartender.

"What's up?"

"As quickly as you can, can you give me five watermelon
martinis and five shots?"

The bartender's brows rose. "What kind of shots?"

"Blowjobs," I said shyly, and the bartender got to work.

I hopped off the stool and went over to the five guys.

"Hey, boys," I said. "I've seen you guys around, haven't I?
I'm Toby, who are you?"

The transition must've jolted them all, and they turned and
were sizing me up. The one who was accused of being the drink
stealer spoke first. "What do you want?"

"To help, of course. See, I think if you all don't stop this,

Atlas will come in, see you all acting like raging morons—no offense—and kick you out for good." I leaned into them and spoke softer. "And then what're you gonna do, drink at Vick's Tricks?" I shuddered.

"Yeah, well, he stole my drink."

"He stole my man."

They went at it again, and I looked over my shoulder, where the bartender was signaling to a tray. I went over quickly, took the tray, and went back to the guys.

"Okay, how about this?" I shouted over them. "My treat. A free drink and shot each."

They looked at the tray, then at me. "Free?" one asked.

"Free. *But*, you guys have to agree to stay on separate sides of the club, and if you don't, Bouncer Man here will tell Atlas you were disrespecting his place." The bouncer in question smirked.

I placed the tray down, glad when they each took a drink and a shot. "Excellent. Now do the shot together. Come on. Teamwork makes the dreamwork."

They chuckled, counted to three, and took the shot. Afterward they all seemed better, and I breathed a sigh of relief when they dispersed.

"Not bad," the bouncer said.

"I'm impressed." The sound of Atlas's voice had me spinning around. "How'd you learn to extinguish an argument like that?"

"I've worked a few places where it was either get a punch or take a blowjob." My eyes widened when Max and Atlas laughed. "I mean the shot."

Atlas, nodded slowly, eyes raking over my body. "Too bad."

Wait, what? Too bad he wanted a blowjob as in physical— what? Wait…

"Max, make sure Toby isn't charged for those drinks. Toby, let me ask you a few questions. Can you come upstairs to one of my VIP booths and talk for a few minutes?"

He was asking me to spend more time with him? What idiot would say no? "Yes."

It was quiet on the second floor, and I knew Atlas likely didn't have any VIPs here yet or wasn't entertaining any. I loved the second floor, and while I'd never been up there, I'd seen it from the first floor. The railing went all around the club, so people could view everything happening down below. And from my usual perch at the bar, I saw the twinkling curtains, and someone once said it was like each area was your own oasis.

"In here." Atlas pulled back a curtain, and I stepped in. There was a black lush couch, glass circular table, a phone I imagined allowed people to call the bar to have things sent up, and dim lighting. *How'd Vick think he could compete with this?*

"Have a seat."

The couch was as soft as it looked, and when Atlas sat beside me, a smile on his radiant face, I couldn't help but mirror it. "This is really nice." I patted the couch.

"Is this the first time you've been up here?" I nodded. "Huh. Well, not the last, I'm sure."

What did he mean by that? I wanted to ask but instead I said, "I only interfered with that altercation because you were short-handed, and I knew after dealing with one fight, you wouldn't want to deal with another. I'm sorry if I overstepped."

When Atlas placed his hand on my knee, I swear I felt that warmth through my entire being. Sure, Atlas was a stunning man. To the naked eye he appeared flawless. Smooth, dark skin, shiny long braids, whiskey eyes that told of tales both good and bad. His smile was like a promise you didn't understand but wanted to kiss until you did. Night after night, he brought joy to people, and while there was no way he didn't know his own appeal, he gave off the impression he was as average as the rest of us.

"Toby, I appreciate what you did more than I can say. This place means the world to me, and I'm very protective of it." He sat back, and I missed his touch. "You've been coming here a while. Ciro and Max know you well. Both speak highly of you and I can say, after having the opportunity to talk with you as well, I'd like to offer you a job as floor manager." I went to speak but he stopped me. "DJ Edge needs a say, but I think he'll agree too. You showed amazing initiative defusing that argument, and I know a natural when I see it."

"Oh wow, Atlas, I'm…" Speechless? Terrified? "But I have a job."

"Are you happy there?"

I knew I wasn't, and I was sure the dislike showed on my face. "It's complicated."

He tilted his head slightly, eyes still on me. "I see. Well, how about you think about it? I'll ask for an answer by Monday. If you turn it down, I'll understand, but I hope you don't."

I wanted to jump on his lap and kiss him in thanks. I wanted to say yes right now, but a lot stopped me. Mostly what Vick would do to me if I left.

"I'll let you know by Monday. Thank you so much."

With that, Atlas got up and left. I watched him walk away, equal parts excited and worried, wondering if it would all work out.

CHAPTER NINE

Atlas

It was an absolutely gorgeous April morning—no rain, the sun was bright, and there wasn't even a chill in the air. The farmers market started up the past week, and I hadn't been able to go, so I decided I would head on over. There was a stand I always visited while the market was up that sold the tea-tree oil shampoo I loved and my favorite sheen oil. I'd buy close to ten bottles through the spring and summer and make it last until the following year.

With my recyclable bags in hand, I walked over, not missing out on some exercise and fresh air. The market was in full swing, and I loved how everyone came out for it. As I perused all the items, I kept thinking about last night.

Seeing Toby masterfully handle the budding brawl was something I'd never expected. Up until that moment, he'd seemed very hesitant of anything new. While he'd danced beautifully up on the stage the other evening, it took him a long time to come out of his shell, but watching him break through was beautiful, and I wasn't fool enough to deny that. Returning to the club and seeing him defuse an escalating situation so seamlessly made a light go off in my head. He had that gift of knowing people, seeing a problem, and figuring out how to alter it for the better. It was rare, and not many people had that in them. And damned if that wasn't hot as fuck too.

One look from Max and I knew he was on board. Ciro wouldn't be an issue at all, and while I anticipated zero argument from Ledger, I was still going to talk with him. I left him a text, since that was his preferable way of talking, and explained my idea to offer Toby the job. I got a thumbs-up, and that was all I needed…well, not all. I needed Toby to say yes.

"Good morning, Atlas. So good to see you this year," Gladys, the woman who sold herbs, said, breaking me from my daydream.

"I was upset not to make it last week. How about some of your fresh basil and mint?"

She smiled and began pulling out tied-up bunches. "How much do you need?"

"Max likes them for some specialty drinks. Just give me enough for the week. I'll be back next Sunday for what I'm sure will be different herbs."

She handed me ten bunches of each; I paid and went to the next stand. That was how I spent my Sunday morning and early afternoon. I found myself checking the club's voice mail to see if Toby called, but he hadn't. And as the sun set Sunday evening, I was beginning to think I might not hear from him.

———

"Did you order a shit-ton of water?" Ledger asked me Monday morning as soon as I entered the club. I'd just come in from outside, enjoying the sunny day, only to walk in to this?

"What are you talking about?" Shaking my head, I moved toward my office, Ledger hot on my tail.

"I'm serious. A truck arrived like fifteen minutes ago with metal barrels of water. I asked what it was, and he said, and I quote, 'a shit-ton of water.' Now, I don't think we order water by the barrel, but I also have no fucking idea."

I opened my office door, flicked on the light, and turned. "I don't usually control the inventory, did you ask Max?"

"I called Max. He said it sounded weird, so you or maybe Keith, the guy who quit, must've done it."

I rolled my eyes and sat at my desk, waking up my computer. "I don't know why I haven't fired him yet. He was giving Keith, his fucktoy, the ability to order shit?"

Ledger cackled and sat down in the chair in front of me. "You're invested in the bond, man. Like we all are."

I knew he was right. Max, Ciro, and Ledger were like my family, and I put up with more than I would from anyone else when it came to those three.

"It says here an order was placed two weeks ago for barrels, yes I said barrels, of water." I read the order form Ledger handed me. "I don't remember ordering this. Likely Max said we needed to order it for the bar, Keith didn't know how to do anything other than Max, and ordered the wrong thing."

"You have so many whacked-out thoughts, Atlas. You probably had some epiphany and ordered it at like two in the morning, and you're blaming a guy who quit. That's like blaming a fart on a dog." Laughing, Ledger stood up, and I swiftly gave him the finger. "I'll store it. It's water, no big."

He left after that. I wanted to investigate it further, see how much it cost me for this order, but I was interrupted by the phone.

With my eyes still on the screen, I answered. "Atlas Durand."

"Good morning, Atlas. It's Toby St. Claire."

The water order was completely forgotten when I heard Toby speak shyly in my ear; just his voice woke up everything inside me. "Hey ya, Toby. How are you doing?"

"Oh. I'm fine, um. It's Monday, and I promised to call you."

"You did, and I appreciate you keeping that promise. I won't lie, though, I'm nervous to hear your answer." I chuckled, relieved when I heard it mirrored in my ear.

"I'm sorry. I couldn't talk to my boss until yesterday afternoon, and then I had to help my sister. By the time I was done, it felt too late to call."

How the earth hadn't eaten up and spit Toby St. Claire out was a testament to his strength. It had been such a long time since someone intrigued me the way he did. He was tougher than he appeared, and knowing the world hadn't always dealt him a fair hand based on the little he'd told me, made me want him working here more than ever.

"You can call the club anytime. I check the voice mail at all hours."

"Oh. Good to know."

There was a long silence, and I realized he wasn't going to speak. "The suspense is killing me."

"Sorry." He chuckled. "My boss understood what an amazing opportunity this was and knew I'd be a fool to pass it up. He needs to get someone to replace me and asked if it would be okay if I could have Tuesday and Thursday to go in and help train my replacement. Only for a couple of weeks."

This clearly was Toby's roundabout way of telling me yes. But something had me curious.

"I did this out of order, hiring you. Can I ask who your current employer is?"

He released a shaky breath, and I could feel his nerves through the phone. "I work at Vick's Tricks."

Of all the places I thought he'd say he worked, that wasn't one of them. Vick's was a dark, dangerous, drug-infested club. Someone like Toby would feel suffocated there, threatened. I wanted to tell him to leave, not look back, and start here tomorrow. But I knew that wasn't who Toby was.

"Okay, Toby. I'm okay with those stipulations. You'll be able to work there for two days a week to train your replacement."

His loud breath made me smile. "Oh, thank you. I was so nervous you'd say no when you heard where I worked."

"On the contrary, Toby. I don't think you belong in a place like that. You are perfect for Joker's Sin."

"Thanks for saying that."

"Can you come in today to fill out some paperwork and talk salary, so you can start first thing Wednesday?"

"Oh…"

I didn't know why that was such a hard question to answer, but I listened while Toby started a sentence a few times. Finally, after the fifth try, he was able to get it out.

"Is around noon okay?" I peered at the clock; it was nine now, and that gave me plenty of time to get the paperwork together.

"That'll be perfect. See you then, and welcome aboard, Toby."

I hung up with a smile on my face and turned to my computer. I shut the program I was using and immediately started gathering the paperwork for Toby's employ.

CHAPTER TEN

Toby

I'd had such an amazing time at Joker's Sin, I almost forgot I had to meet with Vick and tell him how it went and what I'd learned. Sunday morning, as I sat at the kitchen table drinking my coffee, my sister came in and immediately knew something was up.

"Care to tell me what has you looking so upset?" She got her own coffee and joined me.

"Atlas offered me a job, Vick wants me to meet him today to tell him if I got any information on Joker's Sin from my dinner, and I know if I tell Vick about the job, he won't take it well."

Poppy watched me, drinking slowly, assessing. This was how she absorbed any type of shitty news.

"Toby, I have an idea." She placed her mug down and reached over, taking my hand in hers. "I know Vick Keller is a bad man. I hated when you got that job, and I know leaving him is never easy. He's not exactly an equal-opportunity man. But you know what else I know?"

I shook my head, not having a single idea where she was going with this.

"I know Atlas is a big name in Haven Hart. I know Ciro likes you as much as that man can." She chuckled. "I know if you talked to Atlas and told him the truth, now, he might be able to help you."

In a perfect world… "Poppy, you may be right. But if you're wrong, I could end up in the hospital, or dead, and Atlas and all them might also. You want me to risk their lives on a chance?"

She sighed and released my hand. "I want you to be happy and safe, Toby; that's what I want."

"I know. I'm gonna meet with Vick, tell him everything, and deal with the aftermath." I sounded resolute even though my whole body was vibrating in fear.

"Call me after you talk with him. If I don't hear from you, I will call the police." Her gaze flickered with worry, and I wished I could take it all away.

———

I ARRIVED at Vick's right as Liberio was opening the side door. No one would be in but him and Vick, so I walked over.

"Vick be seeing you now," Liberio said, and I followed him in.

"Ahh, there's my ace in the hole." Vick stood from his desk, came over, and slapped my shoulder. "Liberio, get us some coffee. Sit, Toby, and tell me all about your night." He moved back to his chair.

Like a Band-Aid, I'd just rip it off. "Well, there's sadly not too much to say, Vick. He's not an easy guy to figure out. I tried to be subtle so he wouldn't think anything was up, but all he said was that his club was named after someone he knew but didn't give me the name." That was partially the truth, so it came out easily.

"I wanted to get more information, but there was a brawl outside the club."

"I'm disappointed, Toby."

Liberio came in with our coffees. The second he handed me mine, Vick reached over his desk and smacked it out of my hand. The mug clattered against the wall. Luckily no coffee got on me, but I was shaking.

"Did you even try and fuck him?"

"When would I do that, Vick? There was a fight…" And then I remembered the plan I'd had at the bar. "It was because of that guy Chet or Chiv or whatever his name is. He's always here, you know? He started a fight with Ciro, and that's why Atlas got pulled away. I am sure I'd have more information if that high-as-a-kite idiot hadn't started shit."

Vick narrowed his eyes and turned to Liberio. "When Chester gets in tonight, bring him in here." Liberio nodded and Vick's attention was on me again. "So, you go back and try and seduce him some more."

With a deep breath, I just spit it out. "Actually, after that brawl, I was able to stop another inside the club. Atlas liked how I handled it and offered me a job."

I kept my eyes down, unable to see Vick's expression, not sure I wanted to.

"And what did you tell him?" Vick hissed.

"I said I had to talk to my current employer."

There was a beat of silence before he responded. "Did you tell him who your employer was?"

"No."

"That's smart."

I finally looked up when I heard Vick laugh. He was staring at me, grinning, conniving.

"You're gonna take the job, but you'll tell him you need to work here Tuesdays and Thursdays to train a replacement for two weeks." He sat back in his chair, and I breathed a sigh of relief that he wasn't in hitting distance. "That gives you two weeks to get me something else."

"Two weeks, how am I going to…? What if he doesn't tell me anything?"

He shrugged and got up. I watched as he walked around his desk once again and leaned on it, inches from me. "I have my own plan in the works to help speed along Joker's Sin's demise. Between that and anything you get me, I'm confident we can shut that place down." He leaned closer, his face directly in front of me. "If you don't get something amazing in two weeks, I'll pay your sweet sister a visit. When I'm done with her, she'll need more than a wheelchair to get around."

His words were like ice in my veins. I felt my whole body seize up. "Poppy."

"Yes, your sweet Poppy." He grabbed my chin in a punishing grip. "Don't fuck with me, Toby, and don't get all brave on me. Go to the cops or even tell Atlas any of this? You or they won't get to her fast enough. Until our business is concluded, your sister will have a shadow. It will take one phone call and a second of time to make you sorry you ever crossed me. Got it?"

I wanted to answer, but fear had taken my words prisoner.

"I said, *got it*?" With his other hand he hit me so hard across the face, I saw stars and crumbled to the floor. "Words, Toby!"

"Ye…yes. I got it."

"Good. Now get the fuck out of here, clean up, and call your new boss." He cackled and walked out of his office with Liberio on his heels, leaving me sitting on his floor. Coffee was soaking my pants as I sat in what he spilled earlier, and my cheek throbbed.

I took a second to lift myself up. As quickly as my legs could take me, I rushed out of there and ran to the park. It was a gorgeous Sunday, and there were a lot of people out. Fortunately, they were in their own worlds and didn't pay me any mind. I couldn't go home because Poppy was there working, so I sat on a bench, staring at the fountain for far too long.

The sound of a child's boisterous laughter jolted me from my daydream, and I realized it was late morning. There was no way I could talk to Atlas yet. Noticing my pants had dried, I made my way home. In the reflection of a window I passed, I could see my cheek bruising. I knew Poppy would notice, and I'd have to come up with some story. I couldn't let her know she was in danger.

My life was becoming one lie after another. Everyone I cared about would be in trouble if I didn't do what Vick wanted, and any dream of Atlas being interested in me was going right out the window. Eventually he'd figure out what I was doing there, and he'd never smile my way again.

CHAPTER ELEVEN

Atlas

About five minutes after twelve, there was a knock on my office door. "Come in." I was glad to see that when Toby said noon-ish, he meant it. He offered a small smile, and I waved him in. "Good to see you. Have a seat, and we can get through all this boring paperwork crap."

"Oh, sure, and thank you again for the job offer." He sat down, and I placed papers in front of him. He didn't seem like himself, but then again, I didn't know him very well.

"Not to insult your soon to be ex-employer, but working for Vick can't be all that great. A lot of shady dealings going on there."

He didn't say anything to that, just went straight to filling out the paperwork. I noticed he wasn't making eye contact, and the normal flicker of sunshine I'd seen in his face when he was last here was almost nonexistent.

"Everything okay, Toby?" I asked when he handed me the first form.

"Um…yeah, just always afraid I'll fill this stuff out wrong."

He chuckled listlessly. When he got to the contract part, I stopped him.

"This is the money and benefits part."

"Benefits?" This time he did look up, and there was no hiding an impressive bruise on the side of his face. I could tell he'd tried to cover it up and he'd done a good job, but it was noticeable. Anger swelled inside of me—that someone would hurt a man like Toby made no sense. He was sweet, kind, helpful.

"What happened?"

He seemed confused for a brief second before realization dawned. "Oh, my face?" He waved it off. "I slipped on water in my bathroom and got up close and personal with the doorknob."

I wasn't sure if I believed him….Hell, I knew I didn't believe him. But I knew if I pressed further, he'd most likely shut down. I wasn't his therapist, and he seemed more embarrassed than anything else. I let it go for now.

"I see. Well, then, benefits may come in handy. I offer medical insurance to all full-time employees." I spent the next half hour going over that, and he seemed really shocked that I offered dental and vision. Hell, he was surprised there were benefits at all.

"Wow, this is amazing."

"I take it you don't have any insurance currently?"

"No. I mean my sister does because of…well, yeah, so she's covered. But I don't have any. This is really amazing. Thank you."

He signed and I slipped the next page over. "Salary." His eyes widened.

"That's too much."

What the fuck was Vick paying him? "Not really. As floor manager, you have a lot to do. It's more than just walking around and making sure things are running smoothly. You're the link between servers and the bar. You deal with patrons. If Ciro has an issue, he will talk to you if he can't find me. Ledger—DJ Edge—

he will need to make sure things are timed right. It's a huge job, therefore the pay is high."

"And you think I'm qualified to do this job?" Toby pointed to the contract, and his brows quirked, giving him a disbelieving expression.

"I'm a good judge of character, Toby. I believe we see a person's true nature when they assume nobody is watching or when the heat gets to be too much. You had no idea I was watching you when those guys were acting up. I like to think I saw the real Toby that day." Leaning forward, I tried to give him a reassuring smile. "Don't doubt my offer."

"Wow." He chuckled. "I'm not sure what to really say here. I hope I don't mess up."

I took the contract after he signed. "Nah, you'll be good. I'll be working closely with you for the first couple of weeks, get you familiar with everything. Then when you're ready, I'll step away and watch you fly."

"And how will I know I'm ready?" I hated how unsure he was. This didn't feel like the Toby I spoke to the other day, the one who stopped a brawl with confidence, and the bruise on his cheek was feeling more and more to me like the doorknob was a fist.

"You'll know."

When all the paperwork was squared away, I decided to take Toby on a more extensive tour of Joker's Sin. To be successful in his job, he needed to know everything. Ledger was doing sound checks and said he'd talk to Toby later about what he'd need from him to help things run smoothly every night. Ciro wasn't in yet, but Max was doing inventory in the storage room down the hall, so I took him there.

"Wow, that's a lot of alcohol." Toby inched closer to the boxes, reading them. Max had a system—shelves like a library, orderly boxes, and everything set up alphabetically. "That's a high-end champagne."

"That's mostly VIP stuff. Often, we'll get a rich dude looking to impress a twink, or whatever. We like to help a guy out." I shrugged, knowing it probably sounded like it wasn't on the up-and-up, but everyone needed a wingman, and as long as the people involved were legal and consenting, I was good with that.

"Nice. Poppy, my sister, she loves wine. Always pairing wines with books for her book club."

"Does she have a favorite?" I asked. Max lifted his head, knowing where I was going with this.

Toby was looking over the barrels as he spoke. "She's always saying she loves crisp and citrusy…wow, is that a barrel of whiskey?" He moved closer to it, and I gave Max a signal.

"Yes, that's a special order for a party next week."

Max came over, bottle in hand. "Crisp and citrusy, you say?" I asked Toby, who turned when I tapped him on the shoulder.

"Huh?" He then saw I was handing him a bottle of wine.

"For your sister. Max is good at this, and it was all he had to hear."

"It's Outlot Sauvignon Blanc. Citrusy and crisp. It's a favorite around here actually, and before you go saying no, it's not that expensive." Max rolled his eyes.

"Well, thanks." Toby's smile was small, but that light I enjoyed the other night was beginning to flicker. "She's gonna love it, I'm sure."

Toby left shortly after with a promise to return on Wednesday afternoon at two. I went back to my office and had just closed the door when Max came strolling in.

"Did someone hit him?" Max asked, his face turning red as he spoke. Max was insanely overprotective. He might be a man whore, but he didn't oblige bullying and violence.

"He said he slipped on water and hit his face on a doorknob." There was no hiding my disbelieving tone. "Something happened, and yes, I was worried, but it's not like I can force him to tell me."

"A doorknob makes a circular bruise; that was almost the whole side of his face. We're just gonna act like it's nothing?"

"Max." I placed my hands on his shoulders. "We're gonna be there for him and watch out for him. If or when he's ready to talk, he will."

Max closed his eyes and took a deep breath. "Fine," he ground out. "When's he done working at Vick's?"

"He has to stay on there until next Thursday. So four nights, over the next two weeks. Why?" I moved over to my desk and woke up my computer.

"Vick Keller isn't known to just let his employees go," Max said as he sat down.

"None of them tried to leave to come here before, Max. Look around—I'm not sure even Vick Keller would want to take this place, or me, on."

Max shook his head. "Don't get too high and mighty, Atlas. My mom always told me it's the car you don't see that hits you."

I knew Max was right. I'd lived in Haven Hart for a long time and seen a hell of a lot. Vick Keller was an asshole in a long line of assholes harbored by this town.

CHAPTER TWELVE

Toby

The following afternoon I sat in Vick's office, waiting for him to come in and ask if I'd learned anything. I'd tried to absorb all I could while I was at Joker's Sin, but it wasn't like Atlas was going to unlock the secrets of the universe to me. Honestly, I didn't think there were any. He just ran a successful, clean business.

"Ah, Toby, whatcha got for me?" Vick demanded as he stormed into his office and plopped into his chair.

"Not much, sorry. I filled out paperwork and got a tour, that's all." I winced when he sat forward. I hated how he terrified me.

"Tell me about the paperwork and tour."

"Okay…well, the salary is really high, and he's giving me full benefits. So, I guess that's one reason he has so much success there with his employees." Vick nodded and waved me to go on. "He has a ton of high-end liquors, there's a private party next week, and he had this amazing barrel of whiskey. Not bottles like lots of bars, but a barrel." The smile I wore as I described everything faltered when I met Vick's angry gaze.

"Yeah, fancy over there, huh? Don't get too comfy. When it's ashes and dust, you'll come crawling back here to do what I fucking tell you to do."

"Of course, Vick."

He relaxed in his chair, watching me with a calculating expression. "Find out who the private party is."

"I can try. I…"

"No, Toby. You will do! You're a fucking manager there, just ask! You'll have to know anyway. Don't be a fucking pussy."

"Yeah, okay, sure."

"Good. Now…" He grinned maniacally. "Did your sister like the wine Atlas gave her?"

How'd he know about that? "I…she hasn't tried it yet. How'd you…"

"I told you, her shadow is a cunt hair away from her. I say the word, and she's but a fond memory for you to remember and suffocate on the guilt of how you made her death happen."

How did this become my life? "Can I go work now?"

"Yeah, fuck off."

The bar was beginning to fill with the usual scumbags and delinquents. I knew if Vick really wanted to be successful, he'd need to change his clientele. The people who went to Joker's Sin didn't want to be groped by greasy drunks.

"Hey." Shane sidled up next to me, a bottle of gin in his hand. "After work I want to talk to you, 'kay?" There were too many ears around us, and judging by the expression on Shane's face, he knew something.

"Yeah."

The night was its usual—drunk, loud, and touchy. Vick's wasn't a gay bar, yet I got a lot of sexual offers all night long from men. By the time our shift ended, I was eager to leave and talk to Shane. We were a few blocks from Vick's when he spoke.

"Sandy who works the docks, know him?" I nodded. "Yeah,

he said when he got in this morning, the place was swarming with cops." Shane kept looking behind us as we walked, and it was making me paranoid. "So, yeah, you know Chester, the guy who comes to Vick's a lot?"

"Yeah, he started a fight at Joker's Sin the other night." *And I told Vick about it.*

"Well, Sandy said they found Chester beaten to death and strung up on one of the shipping crates."

Holy shit. "I told Vick…"

"Toby, listen to me." We stopped walking, and Shane turned me to face him. "You got a job at Joker's Sin. I know Vick isn't letting you be there out of the kindness of his heart, but use it. Men like Atlas, like Ciro, they're men people listen to. They can protect you, keep you safe. Don't look back, Toby."

The intensity in Shane's eyes made it hard to breathe. "Vick won't let me, Shane."

"He won't hurt you if he knows Atlas is watching you…"

"He's threatening Poppy. If I go to the cops or tell Atlas, he said he'll kill her. Shane, I don't know what I can do."

After a beat, we started walking again. "I'll keep my ears and eyes open at Vick's, see if I can find out who he's using to watch her. If we can get them away from her, maybe it's enough for us to hide her and then figure it all out."

"What's all this 'we,' Shane? He'll kill you."

The bus stop where Shane and I would split up was a block away. "Ever get tired of the shit, Toby? Tired of the heavy hands and puppet strings?" Shane took a breath and smiled. "Put a good word in for me with Atlas, and maybe after all this is over, if we're still breathing, I can work for someone who I wouldn't mind tugging me along."

"Okay, yeah."

Shane's bus pulled into the station, and I watched until he was inside and it was driving away. I decided to walk home; it was a nice night anyway.

I'd just turned the corner to my street when I collided with a wall—no not a wall, a body.

"Shit, I'm sorry." I knew that voice, and when I looked up into honey-brown eyes, I smiled like a dork.

"Atlas?"

"Toby, hey, what are you doing, taking a stroll at night?" He chuckled.

"No, walking home after work. It's a nice night, and my friend takes the bus. I walked him." Why was I rambling? "Aren't you supposed to be at Joker's Sin?"

He nodded. "Yeah, I had a meeting actually, a dinner meeting that ran late, and was just on my way back."

"Ah, okay. Well, I won't keep you. Have a good night, Atlas." I went to move around him, but he blocked my steps.

"I've got time, want to grab a coffee?" He pointed his thumb to the right, where the café bookstore, Quirks and Perks, was still open.

"Oh yeah, that would be nice. Are you sure?"

"Wouldn't have asked if I wasn't."

We walked over, and my heart flipped when he held the door open for me. Such a simple gesture that he probably did for everyone but there were so few kindnesses in the world these days, I took what I could.

"Thanks."

We each ordered a regular coffee, and I followed Atlas to a booth.

"How was work tonight?" he asked as he blew on his coffee before taking a tentative sip.

"Fine, the usual."

"And tell me, what's the usual? I've never been inside Vick's Tricks."

Part of me wanted to tell Atlas it wasn't so bad just so he wouldn't feel bad for me or that I wouldn't be embarrassed for admitting I worked in that cesspool, but I was doing enough lying these days.

"It's pretty terrible. Too many handsy drunks and no one policing any of it. I'll be glad when I'm completely out of there."

Atlas hummed as he took another sip of his coffee. "I've seen so many places come and go in Haven Hart, I'm shocked Vick's is still up."

I heard that a lot. I had a feeling Vick supplied the cops with extra funds to turn a blind eye, but I didn't voice that.

"My friend Shane is there; hopefully he'll find a job after I'm gone. I hate leaving him there. We watch out for each other." I was so focused on the amazing coffee I had, I didn't realize Atlas was staring at me until I looked up. "What?"

"You talk like you work in a war zone. Why do you have to have each other's backs at work? Sure, I will protect my men every day of the week, but there's never a danger that their lives are in trouble. Is that what it's like there?"

Shit. Fuck. I didn't want Atlas getting involved in it. "No, it's fine. Don't worry. I wouldn't stay in a place that was a risk to my life. I swear."

Great, more lies. I was getting way too good at them now.

"You can talk to me anytime, Toby, about anything. If you need help or—"

"No, I'm good. Honest." Atlas gave a curt nod, and I knew he didn't believe me, but I couldn't risk it all.

CHAPTER THIRTEEN

Atlas

After coffee, I asked if Toby wanted to come with me to Joker's Sin. When he readily agreed with a smile, I was glad my place brought him as much joy as it brought me. I realized I really wanted him to always feel that way about the club.

There was still a small line even though closing time was in an hour. Everyone was calling my name, and I smiled and said hello, but I wanted to get inside. Ciro moved, and Toby and I entered the club. Ledger had the place bopping, and the stage was filled with writhing bodies. It was electric when I walked the floor. People respected my space but as I drifted through, fingers and hands glided over my arms, back, and occasionally my ass, I absorbed it all. I never minded; it connected us. Joker's Sin was spiritual for me.

"Busy for a Tuesday," Toby said over the music. I nodded and gestured for him to follow me.

"Hey, Toby," Max slid me over a glass of water. "Want a drink?"

"Oh, no thanks. I have to get home soon, just wanted to see what a Tuesday looked like."

Max didn't say anything more as he moved on to the next person waiting for a beverage. I took the moment, with Toby's gaze roaming over the place, to watch him. He was a beautiful man—troubled, fragile, yet strong. I could see there was a storm raging behind those inquisitive eyes. I didn't know what exactly it was about Toby that pulled me closer to him, but I understood his search. The secrets that swirled through his head, the desperate need to find purity in the dankness that slithered through the streets of Haven Hart.

Building Joker's Sin, creating my mecca, became a beacon for so many, and I found myself hoping Toby felt peace here too.

Toby turned and when our eyes met, there was a crackle in the air. I breathed in the ozone and swam in the intoxicating moment.

"Dance with me, Toby." I put my glass down, took his hand, and didn't give him a chance to think about it.

I crushed his body close to mine, and we melded together. Forward, shuffle, spin, we were in sync. *Fuck.* I'd never felt such a connection when I danced with someone as I did with Toby. Every inch of his body fit mine. His smell, his breath…fucking magic.

Right there on the floor, with everyone watching, our bodies turned sinful. I lifted him up, and Toby wrapped his legs around my waist. His head flew back, and though I couldn't hear it, I felt his laughter, his freedom. We spun, his arms around my neck. The music was our pulse, we were the flow, and damn, I didn't want this song to ever end.

When the song did end, I carried Toby to a stool and gently placed him down. Leaning in so our faces were inches apart, I breathed him in.

"You're addictive, Toby," I whispered.

"Me?" He blinked, his expression disbelieving.

"Mmm." Tenderly I kissed his cheek before standing. "Thanks for the dance; that'll keep me warm for a while."

Toby opened and closed his mouth a few times. Poor guy, did no one ever tell him how stunning he was?

"Get home, safe, Toby. See you tomorrow." It took everything for me to walk away from him but if I didn't, there'd be a positively indecent show right there on the bar.

I heard Max shout last call just as I got into my office and closed the door. I didn't stop. I went right to the bathroom; I needed a shower…a cold one.

———

LEDGER and I had decided that since this was Toby's first night working, we'd make sure everyone here knew it. It was gonna be a party. Long after I got home the night before, I sat in bed, thinking about the man who'd crashed into my life. I'd never found myself wanting to be around someone like this. Not since *him*. Not since Joker. It terrified me, but I believed I could be in Toby's orbit without landing. He was searching for something, and I felt like this place could give him what he was looking for.

"I have a great idea," Max said as Ledger and I were talking over some ideas for the night. Toby would be here in half an hour, so we had to hurry.

"What?"

"The water. We can do something with it and make it a show."

Ledger chuckled. "No time to make something to secure the place for water on the stage tonight, Max."

He waved Ledger off. "No shit, numbnuts. I'm thinking Wet Wednesday. You usually do it once a month, and you're due, no? You've slacked the last few. Let's use it."

It wasn't a bad idea. "I like it. The point of the wet part of it is to get people soaked. It's sexy."

"I'll call my friend and see if he can make some shit to have it fall like rain on the stage." Ledger gestured to where the stage lights were.

"I need to make sure it's legal. Shit, not sure we can get it approved and stuff on time." Ledger, Max, and I were squinting at the ceiling, and that was how Toby found us.

"Is there something up there?"

Toby stood there, wearing dark pants and a hot-pink shirt. His makeup was perfect. He was one hell of a sexy sight.

"We're trying to see if we can make it rain in here for a Wet Wednesday." I smiled and when he returned one, it felt like sunshine.

"You'll figure it out." He was so confident, I knew there was no way I wouldn't make it happen.

"I'll make some calls," Ledger said and walked off the stage.

"Ready for your first night?" I hopped off the stage, onto the bar, and onto the floor, standing directly in front of him.

"I'm scared, but excited."

"Good."

We weren't opening for a few hours, so I made sure Toby understood certain codes we had, things to watch for. An hour prior to opening, I had pizza delivered and we all chowed down. Ciro, Ledger, Max, and I always took the time before opening to unwind. Toby was our fourth floor manager in a short time, and I hoped he'd stay with us for a while. He really fit well with my little group.

The rest of security, servers, and bar staff arrived, and I made sure everyone was acquainted with Toby. He received a nice greeting from my staff, and they took their places. It was time. I loved the buzz leading up to the start of the night.

Toby got right to work. He was speaking to servers and bar staff while the place filled up. He had a very nonthreatening demeanor, and he got positive responses from people.

"You gonna watch him all night?" Max asked as I leaned against the bar.

"I might."

"If you fuck him, I will give you so much shit."

I jerked my head so fast, I almost whipped Max in the face with one of my braids. "Excuse me?"

"Oh, come on. You give me so much of your own shit when I do it…"

"Difference is, I'm never unclear with people. I explain how it is. And if I choose to sleep with Toby, that's not your business."

Max put his hands up. "Chill. I meant nothing by it. I like Toby. Kid's been through shit…maybe still going through it. Even I wouldn't touch him."

I hated how right Max was, but that didn't stop my body from coming alive when Toby was near.

"You have a customer." I pointed at the two guys winking at me, Max went to work, and I watched Toby until it became busy enough to get the party started.

CHAPTER FOURTEEN

Toby

For a good part of the night, I felt intimidated. So many people were moving around, laughing, drinking. Every sound of glass hitting glass made me think there was a brawl happening like at Vick's. But it was cheers—people clinking glasses together to toast something. While at Vick's, hand jobs at the booths were a regular thing, no more than kissing and some dance-humping was happening here. I saw a security guy stop what could've been an R-rated make-out session, but for the most part it was tame.

I'd walked the floor and kept things running as smooth as I could for a good few hours. Atlas wasn't hovering, but he checked on me periodically. I realized it had been a while since we spoke when I heard his booming voice coming from the stage.

"Good evening, everyone."

As usual, the place erupted in shouts, clapping, and Atlas's name echoing through the room.

"It's a special night tonight, and before you all go wondering how it is you have no idea what I'm talking about, I will say it wasn't on the website."

Atlas hadn't spoken to me about anything special happening tonight, and I realized maybe I was supposed to take the initiative to find these things out.

"It's special because Joker's Sin has become complete. We have added to our ranks."

Oh, shit. It hit me like a ton of bricks—I was going to be embarrassed a million times over.

"We have a new manager among us. He will be making sure things on the floor run smoothly, and he's not an unfamiliar face. You all may even remember him from a certain dance competition."

At that moment, people who were around me started looking, and some patted me on the back.

"Toby, where are you?" Atlas asked, and the people started to part. *Traitors.* "There you are, spotlight please?" Ledger did his thing, and suddenly a bright light was on me. "Come on up here."

I knew, deep, deep—like so deep in my soul—that working here, I should be prepared to stand on the stage. But I'd hoped I'd be warned in advance. Atlas and I were going to have to make time for a little talk about this.

Like a man headed for a gauntlet, I made my way onto the stage, unknowing what Atlas had in mind. When I passed DJ Edge, he winked and silently chuckled. I didn't think this was going to be embarrassing, and in no way did I feel I was being set up. But that didn't stop the raging butterflies as I got closer to Atlas…or maybe it was just being close to Atlas.

"There's the man of the hour." Atlas wrapped his arm around my shoulder. "I stole this lovely man from Vick's Tricks." Atlas said it conspiratorially, and the crowd all oooohed at the same time. "I dunno, folks, I'm not sure I'd've just let him go."

My eyes darted up to meet Atlas's. They twinkled with joy,

sure, but there was a heated spark to them and… *No, I'm imagining things.*

"Here at Joker's Sin we like to welcome new family with a lot of flair…" The lights began to circulate all over the room, practically turning the entire place into a light show. "A lot of shine…" Glittery confetti started falling from above, making me giggle. "And of course, a show."

At that, the beginning notes of "Dance Monkey" by Tones and I began and men, clad in white suits with words written all over them, started a choreographed dance. It was incredible. Atlas joined them as if he was born to know their routine. I'm sure I should've felt like an idiot just standing there, but I was so lost in the entertainers. As they moved, I read some of the black words on their clothes: dance, love, accept, move, breathe, embrace. It was so incredible.

I couldn't help but absorb the whole scene before me. I swayed, unable not to feel possessed by the throb of the music. Atlas was amazing as he slid across the stage, landing right in front of me.

"Welcome home, Toby." He spoke into the mic, and the whole place shouted, "Welcome home, Toby." I couldn't remember the last time I laughed and felt so free.

———

"DETAILS," Poppy said the second I entered our apartment. "How was your first day?"

"Shit, Poppy, it's almost three in the morning, why are you still up?" She'd never been up when I came home from Vick's. It was as if she didn't want to know about anything that happened there.

For the next twenty minutes or so, I sat in our too-small living room and told her all about the fanfare and happenings of my first night. She stopped me every few minutes to ask a question, and I admitted to never being as happy with my life as I was when I was working there.

"And you have to work at Vick's tomorrow, right?" Her smiling face dropped as she asked.

"Yeah. But only three more nights doing that, right?" I didn't want to tell her that after those nights, there was no way Vick would let me leave.

"It's going to be okay." She squeezed my hand, and I felt how much she loved me.

I was curious about her day and hoped maybe she'd mention someone following her, and if she could describe them, maybe I'd know who they were. But she said it was a day of work, and then she had lunch with one of her book club friends and that was it. Nothing weird. I wondered for a brief moment if Vick was fucking with me just to scare me and no one was really shadowing Poppy at all.

———

WHEN I STEPPED into Vick's office the following afternoon, I didn't even get to say hello before he gripped my shirt and slammed me against the wall.

"It's funny to stand up there on that fucking faggot's stage and let him make fun of me and my place? You think him getting all his little fairy friends to ooooh and ahhhh over stealing you from me is entertainment?"

Seemed like he was also watching me, which I should've known, but what could I say? My back was throbbing, and he wasn't loosening his grip.

"I can't control what he says, Vick, and if I defended you, do you really think he'd tell me anything?" It sounded logical, and Vick must have agreed, since he let me go a second later.

"You better have something amazing to tell me today, then. Did you find out about the private party?"

I shook my head and winced when he slapped his hand hard next to my ear.

"Tell me something, Toby, or I swear to fucking Christ, you'll regret it."

"I know that he's working on something for Wet Wednesday, and the storage closet has high-end liquor, and there are professional dancers, and Max makes a new drink every night." It all seemed so small, but when Vick smiled brightly and laughed hard enough that he was gasping for air, it suddenly didn't feel so small after all.

"That's perfect. Tell me about this Wet Wednesday, and what sort of drinks does Max make?"

"All I know is, Ledger had to make phone calls to figure out legalities and such for Wednesday, and Max makes new drinks from fresh stuff from the farmers market, or wherever it is he orders stuff."

Gently Vick patted my cheek. "Good work, Toby. This is very good news."

I had no idea how a phenomenal show that Atlas was surely going to put on or information about Max's drinks was at all good for Vick, but I wasn't complaining. I simply left his office and worked through my shift on autopilot. Shane wasn't working tonight, so I had this new girl who didn't know soda from water, and it kept me busy until I clocked out.

CHAPTER FIFTEEN

Atlas

The rest of the week, Toby was perfect. Everything was running smoothly, and there were no complaints. Max, Ciro, and Ledger said they encountered zero issues and a staff meeting with the servers and security all said he was a natural. I was glad since that private party was Friday night and the following week, we had Wet Wednesday. I didn't need any issues.

"This bachelor party on Friday, they're taking up the VIP floor. Why not the private room?" Max asked as we all sat down for our weekly managers' meeting. The weather was wicked, causing Toby to run a little late.

"Max, they are paying a ridiculous amount of money; closing the floor for one night isn't an issue."

"Who are they, again?" Ledger asked right when Toby walked in.

"Sorry I'm late. The rain is awful out there. It just wouldn't let up so I had to bus it, but I missed the first bus so I had to wait."

"No worries, next time let one of us know, and we can pick

you up. There's coffee and bagels. Get settled—we were just talking about the private party on Friday night."

Toby's head whipped around, his color drained, and he was suddenly as pale as a ghost. "Who…um, who's the private party, and um, what will I be doing?"

Maybe he was just nervous, but it was an odd reaction. "Senator Ramos's son, Sam, and his fiancé, Jeremy, are having a joint bachelor party here. It's huge because I've never hosted a political anything, so it has to go flawlessly."

Toby plopped down on his seat, gripping his coffee cup like a lifeline. "Senator?"

"Yeah, Toby, are you okay? I will most likely be hands on for this and leave you to the main floor. Knowing your eyes are on everything else is a huge relief. I can concentrate on Sam and Jeremy."

"Oh…yeah, fine, sorry just." He swallowed loudly. "Senator."

"No shit, right," Max said with a loud laugh. "Next thing you know, Joker's Sin will have celebrities and who knows what else."

We spoke a while about the party, and the whole time, Toby couldn't seem to make eye contact. Only after we moved on and began discussing the rest of the week did he relax and start contributing. I couldn't understand why Toby was so nervous about the party—I let him off the hook. I'd make sure to talk to him alone later.

"We doing a theme day this week then or no?" Ciro asked, wanting to know what to watch for coming in.

"You can't ignore the rest of the week because of the party. Why not a leather night on Thursday?" Max said, and that seemed like a great idea.

"I'll put it on the website."

"You can also, maybe, as a surprise on Tuesday, have like a singles shot night," Toby added. "Since Thursday is so far away, for fun, every single person gets a free shot or something. That can be advertised on the site now."

It was a cute idea and he was right—we did need to do something before Thursday. "Great idea. Too bad you won't be here for that or leather night."

It was the last week Toby would be working at Vick's, and I was relieved he'd be done with the place.

"Yeah, but I'll be there for the party."

The party that terrified Toby. "That you will."

We shot the shit for a little while longer until everyone finished their bagels and coffee; then Max and Ciro said they were going home and would return by the time we opened. Ledger was "going to do music things."

"Toby." I wanted to get him before he had a chance to leave. "If you're not busy, I'd like to talk with you?"

"Oh, well, I have a few errands to do before work tonight. Is there any way we could do it later?"

I didn't think Toby was deliberately avoiding me; he likely did have errands, but I didn't want to talk about this while trying to focus on the club.

"How about you meet me at the diner on Fifth at one? We can get a bite while we're at it. Would you be able to do that?"

He looked at his phone. "It's ten now, yeah, I can do that. See you then."

"Great, see you then."

———

BY THE TIME one came around, I was glad to see the sun was peeking through and was able to walk the few blocks to Fifth to meet Toby. Cindy, who worked at the diner, led me to a booth, and I made sure to face the door so when Toby arrived I wouldn't miss him.

I watched out the window and happened to see the moment Toby stepped off the bus. He had a large paper bag in his hands and was headed my way. He appeared frazzled, probably from doing errands all day in the rain. I felt guilty making him trudge here, but maybe an hour of sitting, relaxing, and eating would calm him down.

He'd just crossed the street when I noticed a man approach him. Toby didn't appear to know the guy and wasn't really speaking, just listening. I noticed that familiar dreaded expression Toby got on his face when something was wrong. I stood to go out and intervene, but no sooner did I make it to the door than the guy walked away. I figured I'd stand by the door at this point, hoping Toby would realize I saw the interaction and talk to me.

"Oh, hey, Atlas, did you just get here?" Toby asked as he stepped into the diner.

"A few minutes ago, I saw you get off the bus, so I figured I'd meet you."

I could tell by his expression and how he swallowed that he was aware I saw the other guy, so I simply asked. "Who was that guy you were talking to? He didn't seem too friendly."

"Excuse me," a lady said, trying to enter the diner.

"Sorry. Toby, our booth is over here." He followed silently and when he sat, setting the paper bag beside him, I waited for him to answer. When he didn't, I nudged. "The guy?"

"Oh, um…he was someone my sister knows. An ex. He startled me is all."

Why is he lying to me? "What did he say? Has he been harassing you and her?"

"What? No, no, it's fine, really, Atlas." He lifted the menu and was reading it over, clearly trying to end the conversation. There was so much secrecy when it came to Toby. While he intrigued me and brought up feelings I'd long hoped were dormant, his lies, his secrecy, brought other darker memories to the surface too.

"Ready to order?" our waitress asked.

We placed our orders, and I decided now was as good a time as any to bring things up.

"Toby, I spoke with the staff and managers, and everyone has the greatest things to say about you. You fit in like you've always belonged."

His cheeks pinked, and the ashen pallor I'd seen adorning his skin too often began to fade.

"Thank you. It's such a relief to hear that. I really felt like it was going well, but you never truly know if people are being nice to you to be polite or if it's genuine."

I agreed with him on that. "You have nothing to worry about there. But one thing you need to understand, Toby, is that I'm good at what I do because I can read a crowd. I can see a person sitting on a barstool and know if they are having a good day or bad one. I can tell when someone looks me in the eyes and tells me half-truths or full-blown lies."

There was the paleness again, and I knew I was on the right track.

"Why don't you start unloading some of that burden that's sitting on your chest? Let me try and help you."

CHAPTER SIXTEEN

Toby

So much of me didn't want to lie to Atlas. I wanted to beg him to help me and wished that if I opened up to him, nothing would happen to Poppy or anyone at Joker's Sin. But the cost was too high; the price was like a noose wrapped around my neck squeezing the choice right out of me. There was no way Atlas was going to settle on me telling him it was his imagination. So, I had to think of something.

"When you offered me this job, I was certain Vick would give me a hard time about taking it. When he didn't, I was waiting for the other shoe to drop."

The waitress came by and quickly placed our meals down, as if she knew we were in the middle of something and didn't want to get involved.

"Go on, Toby." The sincerity in Atlas's brown eyes made my heart ache. Part of me knew if I told him the whole truth, he'd do everything in his power to help me because that was just the man he was.

"Then he told me I needed to work for him for two weeks to train someone." I rolled my eyes, trying to play this whole thing off. "There's been no one to train. And I'm starting to think come Thursday he's not going to let me go."

"Not let you go? He doesn't own you." His voice rose, but he quickly recovered. "I'll come there myself and show Vick Keller he can't own people."

God, I wanted to jump the table, wrap my arms around him, and kiss him senseless. I wanted to thank him for being him. But I couldn't have Atlas doing that.

"No, no, you can't. He may not look like much, but he's not someone to mess with. I'll have to wait it out and see what Thursday brings. No sense in starting something if there's nothing to start, you know?" I dipped a fry in ketchup and ate. Maybe if I stuffed my face, I couldn't talk anymore.

"That's why you've been on edge? The fact that you think Vick will hold you at his place?" I nodded and went on eating even though with each swallow my stomach churned. "That guy back there. He was really your sister's ex?" Again, I nodded because I'd already said so much more than I should.

"Toby, listen to me." When he reached over and took my hand, his skin felt like the remedy to every anguish. "You tell me after work on Thursday what he says, promise. I won't sit by and let him force you to stay there."

I swallowed my food and offered a small smile. *What the hell do I say to that?* "Atlas, you have to understand something. I will never be that person whose decisions harm other people. The guilt I'd feel if something happened to you because of me would be worse than anything Vick could do. I'll be okay." I released my hand from his grip, internally shattered from the loss of his warmth. Even though I knew Vick taking down Joker's Sin would hurt Atlas, he'd still be alive.

"No one should fight a war alone," Atlas whispered, his gaze gravitating toward the view outside. People passing by had Atlas's attention, like any one of them could be a threat.

We finished lunch in relative silence and when it was over, he paid before I had a chance. "I asked you to have lunch with me, don't insult me."

"Well, thanks."

When Atlas and I parted ways outside, I kept thinking about what Vick's guy said to me outside the diner.

"Be careful what you say to Atlas. We will know if you tell him anything."

I knew there was no way they'd be able to hear what I said to Atlas, but they were going to go by whatever Atlas did after our lunch. It was the only reason I even told Atlas what I did. Encouraging him to not go after Vick was a make-or-break moment. Lord only knew what Vick would do to Poppy if Atlas went into Vick's and raised hell. I was convinced he'd wait it out until my last day, so I decided not to let it weigh on me and made my way home to put things away and get ready for work.

———

I shouldn't have been shocked that Monday was just as busy as any other day of the week at Joker's Sin. Obviously Friday and Saturday were the busiest, but the amount of bodies dancing and drinking on a Monday night was amazing. Of course, it had a lot to do with the man himself and not just the drinks. The special Max was offering was bright green. He was calling it Mint Mania.

I watched as Atlas took to the stage and every head in the place turned.

"Hello, my lovelies." His voice boomed, sending a thrill through my body…no doubt many others too. His presence was powerful. "Are you all having a good night?"

He wore an amethyst suit with a black shirt underneath and no tie, so I could see his neck and part of his smooth chest. There was a tiny glint, indicating he had a necklace of some sort on. His braided hair was half up, and I could almost smell his intoxicating cologne from where I stood on the floor. I'd told Poppy his scent was like a magnetic force, and she said something about his natural scent mixing well with whatever he wore, making it uniquely him. I had to agree since I'd never smelled anything so wonderful.

"I was thinking about playing a game," Atlas said, his smile so bright I could see it from across the room. "I need five volunteers, and they need to agree to be blindfolded." While the threat of being blindfolded would have many backing away, in this case the room erupted with people shouting they'd do it.

"Okay, chill, I have some more to say." Atlas laughed. "On top of being blindfolded, you need to be unattached to someone, because what I have in mind very well may make a connection for some of you."

The emotional energy in the place became more seductive with Atlas's further instruction, and DJ Edge began playing some sultry jazz.

"You'll come up on this stage and be blindfolded. Then, I'll stand behind each of you and see who in the room wants to dance with you more. You'll dance with the person I choose, who will *not* be blindfolded, then have drinks.…I will give you both two pieces of cloth. One green and silky smooth, one that will feel rough and be the color red—since one of you will be blindfolded, you'll need to feel the difference. When DJ Edge says time is up, you both will put either the green cloth down on the table or the red one. No fighting. If you both choose the smooth route, you'll be escorted to a private room to have some cocktails, no blindfolds, and get to meet your mystery person."

All I could think was how terrible this would end up at Vick's.

There'd certainly be a bar fight over someone, but I knew this would go smoothly for Atlas.

"Now, who wants to be blindfolded?"

And again, the people cheered.

CHAPTER SEVENTEEN

Atlas

"What the hell, Atlas?" Ledger came storming into my office. It was Tuesday night, the singles shot night was going great, and I'd sequestered myself inside, away from people. I knew why Ledger was angry.

"Shouldn't you be manning the music?" I snapped.

"You fucking well know I have it set to go for a while or else I wouldn't be in here." His eyebrows rose and he pointed right at me. "What's with the attitude?"

"Oh, I'm sorry, Ledger, am I not allowed to have a bad day?" My sarcastic tone wasn't doing me any favors.

"Claude said you snapped at him when he was laughing too loud. Max said you keep telling him to pour faster—"

"I fucking just said I was having a bad day and I came in here, away from everyone. What the fuck else do you want from me?" I was roaring at this point, and it was a good thing the music was loud, and my room was somewhat soundproof.

Ledger plopped down in the chair, staring at me with an unamused glare. "Talk."

I was so pissed, my bones were shaking. My skin was so tight, it felt like it would split at any minute. And I knew why.

"I hate that Toby is at Vick's tonight."

I didn't expect the chuckle from Ledger. "Jealousy?"

"No, worry."

That got a more serious reaction. "What's going on, Atlas?"

I explained to Ledger what Toby had told me at the diner. He didn't seem too shocked about much, but he wasn't thrilled when he heard we needed to wait until Thursday to see how it panned out.

"And what if, come Thursday, Toby is about to leave and Vick...I can't even say it."

"I already thought about it, hence the mood I'm in."

"And let me guess, you offered to go into Vick's and what? Tear him apart?" Ledger smirked.

"I'd do it for any of you guys!"

"Of course you would, you've known us forever. Toby, not so much. So is it that you think Toby can't handle himself or is it you kinda want to handle it for Toby?" The pointed look Ledger shot my way implied a lot.

"I like Toby. He's gorgeous, I won't lie. And the thought of him...yeah, I want to fuck him but—"

"But you care about him and don't want to have to love 'em and leave 'em."

Ledger understood. I'd explained Joker to the guys, and most of them knew the effects that relationship had on me. While they never met Joker, they witnessed my fallout.

"Your inability to care for or even love another person is because of Joker—you still cling to him. You still love him."

"He's dead, Ledger!" I shouted.

Ledger stood and leaned over my desk, face a few inches from mine. "It's lonely loving a ghost, Atlas."

"Are we done here?" I gritted my teeth. Talking about my past wasn't what this was about.

"Yeah." Ledger shook his head. "Maybe we should talk to Ciro about ideas for finding out what Vick has planned, if anything, with Toby."

"Yeah, good idea. I'll talk to him."

"After closing, we'll all sit and talk. Toby's a good guy, and I don't want to see anything happen to him."

I nodded and after Ledger left, I pressed my palms against my eyes. This day was for shit.

After closing, the four of us sat down, and I went over everything with them. None were pleased to hear how worried Toby was over leaving Vick's, but they were all in agreement that just showing up and threatening Vick would be dumb.

"I know Liberio, Vick's main guy. Head full of rocks but he's driven by violence. He takes pleasure in causing pain," Ciro said. "I keep my ear to the ground, I know things. He actually came in here a few times, likely checking the place out."

"Not surprising," I said. I didn't know any club owners that hadn't had people go check out the competition.

"What's the likelihood something will happen to Toby on Thursday?" Max asked.

Ciro gave an uncommitted gesture. "Depends on how okay Vick is with Toby leaving."

"I have a feeling he's had issues with Vick before. Some ending not very cleanly," I said, and they all nodded.

"The bruise on his face." Max voiced what we were all thinking.

"What about if one of us picked him up Thursday night after his shift?" Max tapped the table excitedly. "Or a couple of us. No way Vick would hurt Toby with all of us there."

"And what if he does it like midshift?" Ledger was a thinker and while I was grateful, realizing every idea was met with a brick wall was upsetting.

"I got a guy," Ciro said. "Unassuming friend. He's more of a hacker, but he's like a chameleon. I can have him follow Toby around. Keep an eye on him until we know it's all good."

"You sure Vick won't figure it out?" I had to ask, knowing Vick wasn't a complete idiot.

"Don't you worry." Ciro's confidence was reassuring, and he said he'd call him on his way home and let me know first thing in the morning.

"Should we tell Toby?" Max asked as we all were walking to our cars.

"I wouldn't," Ciro said. "If he knows, he may make it obvious. It would be best if he was kept out of the loop for now."

I didn't like the secrets, but I made a silent promise to myself that after Toby was out of there I'd let him know.

———

WHILE I LIVED in the heart of Haven Hart, I still chose to drive the ten blocks to my apartment. Haven Hart had its good and bad parts, but monsters lurking in the shadows weren't going to go away anytime soon.

I lived in a gorgeous penthouse apartment that took me years to obtain. I always felt like it rested on top of the clouds, and I could look down on Haven Hart, see the bustle, feel it come alive through my veins, but the silence...I loved the silence. Whereas at Joker's Sin the thump and pulse of the music drove me, here the silence balanced things out.

It was late and while I was hungry, all I wanted to do was flop face-first on my bed and pass out.

I stepped into my apartment, tossed my keys into the blue crystal bowl that was on the table by the door, kicked off my shoes, and walked toward the living room. The lights were motion sensitive by design. I didn't like walking in and having to search for lights, but I also wasn't going to waste electricity by keeping them on all night.

The city sparkled as I glanced out my floor-to-ceiling windows on the way to my bedroom. Each step felt like mine, but it also ached with loneliness. None of my one-night stands ever set foot in my place. Max, Ciro, and Ledger were the only three that ever came here, and while that filled the spaces sometimes, I found myself beginning to wonder if coming home to someone would be a welcome change.

Could I let someone in again?

Would I even remember how to love someone like that again?

I shook those thoughts off, got undressed, and did what I wanted to do the second I got home: face-planted on my bed and passed out.

CHAPTER EIGHTEEN

Toby

I tried to do everything in my power to avoid Vick on Tuesday. Shane seemed to sense that and oftentimes would pile on more work for me, so whenever Liberio or Vick came by to talk, I was so busy, they told me they'd find me later. Shane kept asking if I was okay, and I said yes but I wasn't. I knew who the private party was, and I knew Vick would want to know.

Telling him the senator's son and his fiancé were having a bachelor party at Joker's Sin would be huge. It would hopefully be enough, and he might leave Poppy alone. But on the other hand, it could possibly destroy Atlas. I hated this so fucking much.

I thought I might be out of the woods when I saw that my shift was ending in fifteen minutes. Shane told me to go to the bathroom, hang there, and when it was time, he'd clock me out, so I just had to dart out the back door.

I was almost to the bathroom when Liberio blocked my path.

"Vick will see you, come now."

I didn't know much about Liberio. No idea about nationality

or anything. He spoke very little and hardly ever to me. I had zero time to dwell on it because he took my arm in a rather forceful grip and escorted me to Vick's office.

"Oh, Toby, good, I was hoping I'd see you before you left." The narrowing of Vick's eyes and the scowl told me he knew I was avoiding him.

I didn't know what compelled me to snap at him, but I did. "Well, Liberio didn't give me much choice, seeing as he forced me here." And I'd regret that. Vick nodded and Liberio yanked on my arm and punched me in the stomach. The force was so hard, had I eaten I would've thrown up. This must be what people meant when they said they saw stars. When I tried to stand up straight, Liberio tossed me onto the chair, and I tumbled over it and landed on the floor.

"Get the fuck up!" Vick shouted. My body ached but not as badly as I thought it would; it was a little hard to breathe, but I was managing. As I sat in the chair, the bravery I felt a few seconds ago turned to dread. Vick was getting more liberal with the violence when it came to me, and all that did was make me realize I was either stuck there or I wasn't going to get out in one piece…or at all.

"Are you done being a sassy little shit?" I nodded at Vick's question, really not wanting any more hits. "Now, I know when people are avoiding me. It usually means two things. One, they don't have what they owe me. Or they do but are greedy and don't want to give it up. Which is it, Toby?" He held up a hand when I opened my mouth. "And before you answer, know that I'm pretty sure I know which it is."

I had to lie. But maybe I could make him believe me. "So, I actually don't know which it is you think I am but, I was trying to find out who the private party was. I thought it would be on the schedule, but it just said private party. They had a managers' meeting, but I was late because of the bus and missed the info on it." Vick's hands that were resting on the top of his desk, fisted. "I did ask, though. I said I missed it and since I was floor manager, I should know."

"Good thinking." I took the morsel of a compliment and ran with it.

"Except Atlas told me not to worry about it. They were taking the top floor and I'd be running things on the first. He was taking lead on the party, so I'd just have to worry about things below." Not a total lie and maybe just enough truth to get me through this.

"So you don't know who? That's what you're saying? That's why you've been avoiding me?"

Releasing a sigh, I sagged against the chair. The pain from Liberio was starting to register, and I just wanted to go home. "Yes."

"Hmm." Vick sat back, gaze assessing me. "Maybe not a total loss. You said Atlas was leaving the floor to you, yes?"

"Yeah."

"Ciro may be the only speed bump, but I may be able to get around it."

I didn't know what he was talking about, but I knew I wasn't going to like it.

"Here's what's going to happen. Make sure you let me know if Friday's a themed day. I'll get some guys in there. They'll approach you, ask what's the best drink there so you'll know they're my men. You're to turn a blind eye to whatever they do. Get it?"

Oh, this was bad. "But if they do shit that's not allowed, and I do nothing I'll lose my job."

Vick scowled, his face became red, and anger rippled over his skin. "You don't work there, Toby, do you think that's your life now?" He stood and rounded the desk. I moved as fast as I could to get away, but Liberio stopped me. "I'm your boss until I've had enough of you. If Atlas fires you, so the fuck what? You're not gonna be there much longer anyway. Get it?" He pressed his hand against my chest, my back to Liberio's front. "Don't get it in your head that this is a fucking fairy tale and someone's gonna save you. Now get the fuck out of here, and I better have good news come Thursday. When my guys get there, you will let them do what they will be there to do. Or else you, Poppy, and all your fucking dreams will die."

After I was dismissed, I left out the side door. There was no way I wanted to talk to Shane about this. I was actually starting to think I should keep my distance from him. I almost missed the bus but at the last minute jumped on. With my head resting on the cool glass, I shut my eyes and wished my life was a fairy tale and someone would rescue me from it.

Poppy was asleep when I got home, thank goodness. I got myself some water and painkillers and went to the bathroom. I was exhausted and my body was throbbing, but I had to wash it all away. Liberio's and Vick's touches, the smell of stale beer and body odor. All of it. I turned on the shower, popped the pills, divested myself of my clothing, and stepped into the shower. The warm water felt great. I took a moment to check out the damage on my body. My arm had an obvious grip mark that would likely end up black and blue by the next morning. My stomach was pinkish where Liberio punched me, and my hip, yeah, I'd had a feeling when I hit the floor I'd end up with a bruise there too. I was going to be colorful for the next few days. I'd make sure to cover it all up and be aware that I'd be vulnerable there. I didn't need Atlas seeing them and raging. No matter how much I wished he'd come and rescue me, I couldn't chance it.

CHAPTER NINETEEN

Atlas

I didn't even try to hide how anxious I was for Toby to arrive to work on Wednesday. I literally paced the floor. Ledger chuckled into the microphone during sound checks, and Max asked if I wanted a shot or ten. Doors didn't open for another hour, but I knew he'd arrive soon. I needed to see he was okay. Ciro's friend Desi was going to begin keeping an eye on Toby the next day. He'd come into Joker's Sin that night and get a feel for the guy and would make sure to stay with Toby on Thursday while he worked.

"Hey, Atlas." The sound of Toby's voice as he walked in felt like an injection of calmness. I never wanted to hear a voice more than I did right then.

"Oh good, you're here." I wanted to hug him, but I also didn't want it to come off like I didn't think he could've made it this far without me. "Are you okay?"

Toby's bemused expression as he walked around me to get to the coat check area to drop off his things actually made me smile. He wasn't angry, or sad, or anything. He seemed fine.

"I am." He handed the coat to Tex, who was working the coat check. Toby turned, brow raised. "Were you worried about me?"

"I think you know I was, Toby. After our lunch, what you told me."

He gave a curt nod. "Yeah, I know. But I made it through the day, and I'm fine. Just one more shift, right?" He quickly walked over to his little station and began reading the schedules and such.

"Did Vick talk to you? Anything happen?" I felt like a lost puppy. I wasn't a fan of this feeling at all.

He placed the schedule on the podium and granted me a smile—a small one, but a smile all the same. "Of course he did. And I told you I'd tell you how Thursday went and if anything happens when I go to leave. I promised."

He reached over and squeezed my arm. The pressure went all the way down, and I swear it stopped at my cock.

"Toby, after work, let me drive you home?"

He furrowed his brow and his lips quirked adorably. "If you want to, you can drive me."

"Thank you."

The night was uneventful. People drank, laughed, danced, and there was no drama. At one point, Ciro found me and let me know Desi was at the bar, wearing a Beatles shirt, so I made my way over. He was right about Desi being unassuming. He appeared to be average. Brown hair and eyes, kind face, he was drinking a beer and talking with people, but I could tell he was watching Toby the whole time. He was very good, because I didn't think anyone else knew that guy was there for him. Not even Toby. He made eye contact with me but other than that didn't acknowledge I existed. Perfect.

When the doors were closed and the place cleaned up, Toby left to make a quick call and Ciro approached.

"I hear you're driving Toby home?"

"Yeah, I don't think him taking the bus is smart."

Ciro nodded. "Desi's gonna head over to Toby's building. Here's his number, text him when you're leaving here so he knows to watch for you. If he doesn't hear from you in like an hour, he's gonna call me and I'm gonna come lookin' for you." Ciro wasn't threatening me; he was promising, and I knew the big guy with training he wasn't even allowed to talk about had my back.

"Thanks, man."

With everyone gone, I sat at the bar and waited. Which wasn't very long. Toby came strolling by, his stuff in hand and a pained smile.

"Hey. You okay?" I asked and noticed that as he lifted his messenger bag on his shoulder he winced.

"Huh? Oh." His eyes widened for the briefest of seconds, but it was long enough for me to see he meant to hide the pain. "Headache."

"Bullshit."

I stood in front of him, and when I went to relieve him of the messenger bag, he stepped away and cowered slightly. *Did he think I was going to hurt him?*

"Toby, I'm not going to hurt you. I was going to take the bag from you and carry it."

He immediately deflated, slid the bag down, wincing once more, and handed it over. "Thanks."

"It's not a headache, is it?" I shouldered the bag.

"I'm really fine, Atlas, I'm tired though and I want—"

"Show me."

"Atlas, I—"

"Toby." After placing the bag on the bar, I took Toby's hands as slowly and as gently as I could. "Please, show me."

Toby wore a T-shirt with a light hoodie. Even when it got hot in there, he hadn't taken it off. Now, I was kicking myself for not realizing it. He didn't take his eyes off me as he unzipped the hoodie. When it slipped from his arms, he still watched me. Right there on his arm was a bruise. It wrapped around and it was clearly made by a tough grip.

I reached out, and feather-lightly touched it with my finger. When I met his eyes, they were already on mine, as if he didn't want to look at the marks.

"Anywhere else?"

He didn't argue with me, just lifted his shirt, exposing his stomach, another bruise blooming like the one on his arm. Without me asking, he unbuttoned his pants and slid them past his hip, where yet another mark adorned his beautiful skin.

I hoped he couldn't see how I was feeling. It felt like there was fire in my veins; the buzzing in my ears made it hard to think past going to Vick's and beating him within an inch of his life.

"Atlas," Toby's voice was a whisper and when I lifted my gaze to his, tears ran down his cheeks. "I'm okay, I swear."

No. I wasn't brushing this off. "You're not, Toby, you're…" I tenderly pressed my palm to his stomach. He didn't stop me, and he sighed. "You can't go back there."

His head snapped up, golden brown eyes filled with defiance, sadness, and I swear, guilt. "I have one more day."

"It can kill you."

His smile belied how I knew he was feeling. "I always loved coming here, watching you perform. When I would have to work at Vick's, I got through it knowing I'd be rewarding myself by spending Saturday nights here. You didn't really know I existed until Sparkles dragged me up on that stage." He chuckled and as if my body took away my common sense, I wrapped Toby in a hug. "All I ever wanted was for you to see me and now—"

"I do see you, Toby. You mesmerize me."

Toby stepped away, quickly rebuttoning his pants and adjusting his T-shirt. I thought he was going to leave, but I followed him as he walked around the stage to the stairs. "Will you dance with me before we go, Atlas?"

There wasn't a force on Earth that would make me deny him that. I went up the stairs right behind him, and as he stepped onto the stage, I took his hand.

"There's no music," I said.

He shrugged. "I sometimes think you're the music. Hold me, move, and we'll find our rhythm."

Center stage, in a very vacant Joker's Sin, I gently pressed Toby to my body, and we danced.

CHAPTER TWENTY

Toby

Tendrils of happiness, contentment, and desire corded all around me as Atlas danced with me on that empty stage. Unfortunately, there was also guilt. No matter how I swung it, I had been lying to Atlas and as amazing as this bubble I was in was, the second he found out it would burst, and this would be no more.

"Toby," Atlas whispered against my ear. "I don't know what this is I'm feeling, and I can't promise you it'll be anything more than this here. But, I want so much to kiss you right now. Honestly…" he chuckled. "If you weren't hurting, I'd likely seduce you and not let you go until morning."

"Oh, I see how it is," I joked even though my insides were thrumming with excitement. "You don't think I can take a little seducing?" I wanted to tell Atlas I wanted more than a kiss, that I'd dreamed about having a man like him want me and keep me forever. But at the end of the day, I was a liar and if a kiss or one night was all I could get, I'd take it.

"Here's how this is gonna go down, you little minx." His hands gently caressed me, lowered to my ass, and scooped me up carefully. I yelped but immediately wrapped my arms and legs around him. He was so gentle as to not hurt me.

"I'm gonna go right ahead and kiss you breathless for a while, then take you home. You're gonna heal, Toby, because Friday night, after the bachelor party, after everyone is gone, I'm gonna get wicked with you."

Holy shit. "Damn. I'm all for that plan."

Staring into Atlas's lust-filled eyes, I had no idea where he was taking us. I felt the jolt in his steps, so I knew we were walking down the stairs. When we evened out, I pressed my lips to his neck, feeling the hum he released as I tenderly kissed his pulse point.

"Damn," he said, and in a second, my ass was on a cushion. Leaning away, I realized I was on a barstool. "I was gonna go to my office and kiss you a fuckton on my couch, but I'd never stop."

"I keep hearing a lot about this kissing, Atlas. Maybe stop with the talking and—" *Oof.* In an instant, Atlas's arms wrapped around me, and his soft lips pressed against mine. It was like hot meeting cold—thunderous, powerful, jolting in the best way. My hands tangled in his silky braids and his scent, his feel, his every-thing invaded every part of me. I'd wanted to kiss this man forever.

His tongue dipped into my mouth, and I wasn't sure what was here or there, whether it was day or night. I just knew Atlas. At that moment, ensconced in his passion, I felt no pain, felt no anger, sadness, or guilt. I felt happy. Lust poured between us. It was the most fluid kiss anyone had ever given me, and I was greedy enough to take it.

"You taste so sweet," Atlas said, and I didn't get a chance to respond before he was taking my lips once more. I don't know how long we were wrapped around each other, kissing. But when we came up for air, his lips were puffy and his eyes were glazed over. I loved how I'd done that to him.

"I can't wait until Friday night," he said, and I laughed at the pure joy and need in his voice.

"Me too."

"Mmm, okay, let's get you home."

He helped me stand and grabbed my messenger bag from the bar and handed me my hoodie. As we walked out of the club to Atlas's car, he kept his hand on the small of my back and for reasons I couldn't untangle, it anchored me.

The ride home was full of talk about the bachelor party I dreaded, music, and a little bit about my parents. I found myself telling Atlas more about my sister and the accident that put her in a wheelchair. He didn't shoot me looks of pity, just deep understanding of life's pains. My life wasn't a tragedy, no matter what people on the outside might think. Well, I guess it wasn't always a tragedy. Vick Keller was doing a great job of turning it into one.

"Here I am," I said as he pulled up to my place.

"I had a great time tonight, Toby, and I don't mean the hours of work, I meant after-hours."

Smiling I daringly leaned in, thrilled when he gave me a chaste kiss. "Me too. I'll see you Friday."

I knew he was going to say something, but I couldn't bear to hear it. I needed to get out of the car because the moment he smiled and kissed me good-bye, the guilt flooded me.

I was relieved when I went into my apartment and Poppy wasn't around. She was likely asleep or watching TV in her room. I decided I'd shower in the morning and quickly slipped into my room. I plopped onto my bed and closed my eyes. I could smell Atlas's cologne on my hoodie, and that was how I fell asleep, wrapped up in him.

————

As I walked into Vick's Thursday night, I was filled with terror. Atlas had sent me many texts asking me to stay away and not go. Last time I saw Vick, I left black and blue and with a threat that I'd never be done with him. And after showing Atlas my latest bruises, I understood his worry, but I had to go in. There was no choice. Shane saw me and waved from across the bar. I went straight into the kitchen to store my stuff. I just had to hope that when I left after my shift, it would be just as I was then, and hopefully Vick wouldn't need me anymore.

"Last night?" Shane said as he entered the kitchen.

"Right. I don't really think Vick'll let me go." I pushed my messenger bag and cell phone behind the bread, hoping no one stole it.

"Yeah, I've been thinking. Have you talked to Poppy? Asked her if anything weird has been going on?"

"I ask her about her day all the time. Nothing."

"So maybe it is nothing. Maybe Vick is trying to scare you."

I went on to tell him about the diner and how the guy came up to me, knowing I was meeting with Atlas and to say nothing.

"He has ears everywhere, Shane."

"Just be vigilant. And…" he leaned in to whisper. "Maybe see if there's a job opening at Joker's Sin. This place will be shit without you."

I smiled at him. "I promise I will find you something if Atlas doesn't kick me to the curb for lying to him."

"I don't think he will."

We got to work right after that. Same old patrons as always, plus a few new ones. One I swear I'd seen at Joker's Sin before, but that wouldn't shock me at all. I did my job and kept my head down. I kept conversations short and wanted the night to end so I could leave. I knew me leaving without Vick calling me into his office was futile. After the last patron left, Liberio told me to meet Vick in the back. Shane offered me a sympathetic smile, and I walked to what I hoped wasn't my doom.

CHAPTER TWENTY-ONE

Atlas

If it wasn't for Ciro's friend Desi texting him through the night Thursday, and Ciro updating me on things with Toby, I'd have gone crazy. As it was, I was barely hanging on. I tried to sway Toby from working, but his refusal was absolute. There were two hours left until Joker's Sin closed, which meant Toby would be off shift at Vick's right about now. I leaned against the bar, my gaze roaming over the leather-clad bodies moving in rhythm with the music, but I couldn't feel it like I usually did. I felt disconnected. My whole mind was on Toby. I needed to know he was safe.

"Drink this." Max pushed over a brandy snifter. The brown liquid glided and settled. "Your finger-thrumming and pacing, it's not going unnoticed. People come here for you, Atlas. Right now, you're giving off a very unapproachable vibe."

I knew Max was right. I took the brandy and drank it, loving the smooth burn, and when I placed the snifter on the bar, I took a deep breath.

"Better?"

I nodded to Max and decided to walk up to the VIP floor. Less folks there and maybe I could stay off people's radar.

They were all faces I knew, and I spent a few minutes with each making small talk and then sequestered myself in a corner area. I had a view of the entrance, so if Ciro walked through, I'd see. How I was feeling about Toby occupied my thoughts. Relationships were not something I ever wanted.

My phone vibrated in my pocket, and I saw that it was Ciro.

"Hey."

"Where are you?"

"VIP, why?" I was up and making my way to the stairs before I finished talking.

"Desi called. Something's up." The chill that ran down my spine almost had me tripping on the stairs.

"I'll be right out."

I stopped at the bar. "Max." He came over, concern marred his face.

"I gotta go, tell Ledger. You guys close up."

"What's going on?"

"It's Toby. I'll call you when I know more." I didn't stay to hear what he said. I stepped out front. The line was gone since we would be closing soon. Ciro stood next to his car.

"Come on, I'll tell you on the way." He got in the driver's seat and I slid into the passenger's side.

"Where are we going?"

"Desi texted, said Toby was called back to Vick's office after his shift. The place was closing, so Desi had to leave the building but decided to wait outside. He was discreet, but when Toby didn't come out after twenty minutes, he moved to the side entrance. He saw Liberio tossing Toby into a car."

I was digging my nails into the upholstery, I hated where this was going. "Where is he, Ciro?"

"Desi followed in his car and texted me. That's when I called you, but while you were on your way to me he said they drove Toby to his apartment but barely stopped the car before pushing him out."

What the fuck? "Drive faster."

———

WHEN WE PULLED up to Toby's place, there were no cops, no ambulance, nothing. Which meant Toby went up to his apartment in fuck knows what condition.

"You go up, I'll park," Ciro said.

I only knew what floor and number Toby's apartment was because I'd read his paperwork. When I got up to his floor, I saw Desi standing outside his door.

"You had one fucking job," I growled. "Seriously?"

"Atlas, I couldn't follow him back there."

When I was an inch from him, I grabbed the front of his shirt and slammed him against the wall. "You saw Liberio throwing him in the car!"

"And I was outnumbered!"

At this point we were shouting, doors were opening, and Ciro stepped onto the floor.

"Let him go, Atlas. It's not his fault," Ciro said.

"What the hell is going on out here?" The sound of a very irate woman made all of us turn. In a wheelchair, there was no question who she was—Toby's sister. Fraternal, sure, but there was no mistaking she was his twin sister.

"You must be Poppy," I said as I released Desi. "I'm—"

"Atlas, I know who you are. All of Haven Hart knows who you are." She eyed Ciro and Desi. "And who are you fine men of Fight Club?"

"I'm Desi, this is Ciro." Desi stepped closer to Poppy and

while I knew it wasn't his fault Toby was hurt, he was the closest to blame.

"Well, Ciro and Desi, how about you two and Atlas come inside before Gretel two doors down calls the cops." Poppy gave a little wave to someone behind me, no doubt Gretel.

I wanted to see Toby, so I quickly agreed and followed her inside. Their place was small. A living room with an adjoining kitchen. Open plan, which I liked, but with the three of us and Poppy, it felt too small.

"Is Toby here?" I asked.

"Um, I believe I heard him come in. He often showers and passes right out after work, although…" She frowned and glared toward the hallway. "He didn't shower. He always showers after Vick's since he hates the smell. Not after Joker's." She winked at me, but her gaze returned to the hall.

"Would it be okay if I knocked on his bedroom door?" I asked, my whole body vibrating with the need to move past her to Toby's room.

"I suppose that would be fine." She wheeled back, letting me pass, and when I was in front of Toby's door, I was about to knock when I heard it. Crying.

I met Poppy's eyes, and I knew she saw something in my expression, because when I refrained from knocking and just opened the door, she didn't try to stop me.

Toby mustn't have heard me, since he didn't budge when I shut the door. As I got closer to the bed, what I saw nearly broke me.

He was on his side, clutching his pillow. The moonlight shone over his face…his swollen, bruised face. I wanted to scoop him up in my arms, but I knew there was more wrong than what I was seeing. I needed to get him medical attention.

I moved over to the side of the bed, where I knew he'd be able to see me, and kneeled.

"Toby," I whispered.

He hiccupped and lifted his head slowly. His left eye was swollen shut, and his lip was split. Blood painted his pillow, and I had to breathe slowly to stop from storming out of his room, finding Vick, and ending him.

"Atlas?" He narrowed his one good eye. "Oh, God, Atlas."

"What did he do to you?" I reached out, glad he didn't flinch. Blood had crusted against his skin, his hair was matted, and I wanted to weep. I wanted to make Vick pay.

"I'm so sorry, Atlas, I—"

"Shh. No, don't be sorry. But, Toby, we need to get you to the hospital."

"No…" He started sobbing again. "Leave me, I deserve it—"

"Stop." I didn't like snapping at him, but I wasn't going to let Toby break himself. "We need to get you to the hospital, but I'm afraid to touch you, so I'm calling an ambulance."

He started to say something, but I stopped him. "No. Listen, don't speak. We tried it your way. Now I'm taking over. Hospital first. No arguments. We'll talk after." Leaning over, I pressed a kiss to his forehead, and his skin tasted like copper. "I have to talk to your sister too."

"Poppy, no wait, she's in danger—"

"She won't leave our side. I have Ciro and another guy here. We won't let anything happen to her. Please, Toby. Let me lead here."

"Like a dance," he whispered, his voice hoarse from crying.

"Yeah, baby, like a dance."

CHAPTER TWENTY-TWO

Toby

I could hear Atlas moving around, talking. I also heard Poppy and crying. I decided to rest my throbbing head and wait. I didn't have much choice in trusting Atlas, but at the same time I wanted to. I didn't deserve his help and his worry, but I was just so tired.

As they all talked and the world moved on around me, I replayed everything that happened at Vick's. He'd once again asked about the private party that was happening on Friday; it was the first thing out of his mouth. When I said I didn't know, I watched as Vick's face turned from his usual scorn to violent.

After that, it was something out of my worst nightmare. Liberio had grabbed my arms and held me. Vick shouted that I was a liar, that he knew about the senator's son and fiancé and if he knew, then I did. He told me he no longer trusted me and that Poppy would pay the price for my deceit. That was when I reacted. With his face so close to me, I head-butted him and blood poured from his nose.

After that it was a series of punches, pain bloomed behind my eyes, and Liberio pulled me so hard, my shoulder dislocated and I heard the pop. When I was on the ground, trying to breathe, I heard Liberio telling Vick he'd drop him at my apartment and handle Poppy when she left our place. I tried to speak but was met with a kick.

Liberio lifted me and I could barely walk on my own, so some other guy helped, and it was such a blur after that. I knew I was at my place when I was tossed out of the car, and I got up close and personal with concrete. It was so late, not many people lingered and as quickly as I could, pain radiating through my body, I made it to my apartment. I could hear Poppy's television on in her room, so I quickly slipped into mine and collapsed onto my bed.

"Mr. St. Claire, can you hear me?" There was a light shining in my eye. I think I made a grunt of some sort. "We need to move him off the bed," the woman said.

They began doing whatever it was they did, I heard myself scream when they moved me, and Atlas yelled at them to give me something for the pain.

"Mr. Durand, please move and let us do our job." I didn't hear Atlas's response because at that moment, I passed out.

———

WHEN I OPENED my eyes again—well only the one, the other wouldn't cooperate—I knew I was in the hospital. What I didn't know was how long I'd been there. I didn't dare move as right that second, I felt no pain and shockingly, I wasn't disoriented. I knew what had happened to me, and I knew I needed to talk to Atlas.

As carefully as I could, I looked around the room. The bed was slightly elevated, so I was able to make out enough to see that two people were there. Poppy and some other guy I assumed was someone Atlas knew.

"Poppy," I whispered, my throat feeling like it was on fire. She wheeled over quickly, and her warm hand immediately took mine.

"Jesus, Toby, you scared the ever-loving shit out of me." Her eyes were red and puffy from crying.

"I'm sorry, Poppy, I didn't mean to."

I knew if I wasn't laid up in a hospital bed, injured, she'd have smacked me.

"Let me get the nurse." She went to move when the other guy walked up to the bed.

"Stay, Poppy. I'll get her." He met my eyes briefly before stepping out of the room.

"We could've just hit the button," I said.

"I think Desi is giving us a second. Toby, do you remember what happened? I mean, there's no wondering who did this or anything, but the cops are going to want to talk to you."

So many cops worked for Vick, there was no way to know who would show up and if they were on his payroll.

"Poppy, I can't. He owns a lot of the cops." I started coughing, and that pain I was trying to avoid came at me full force.

"Okay, no more of that," a nurse said as she walked in, Desi behind her. "Good to see you're up."

"What…what day is it?"

"Friday, two fifteen in the afternoon," she said with a smile as she started checking my vitals.

"Atlas. I need to talk to him."

Poppy smiled and squeezed my hand gently. "He has a huge party tonight. He was actually going to cancel it, but I knew you'd be angry if he did, so with Desi and Ciro's help we convinced him to go. He said right after that you and he had a promised date."

Shit. "Poppy, listen…"

"Mr. St. Claire, the doctor will be in shortly. I have some painkillers for you, and I want to change the ice on your shoulder. It was dislocated, and keeping the swelling down is key. You can't move it because it's in a shoulder immobilizer."

"Okay, thank you, but…"

"Just sit tight, dear, he'll be here in a moment." After she injected what I assumed was the pain meds into my IV, she left, and I met Desi's watchful eyes.

"Desi, right?" He nodded. "You need to call Atlas, tell him he needs to cancel tonight. He has to!"

"Toby, what's this about? He said he'd be here at the end of the night." Poppy brushed the hair from my eyes and gently kissed my hand.

"Why, Toby?" Desi asked.

"Vick knew about the party tonight. Who it was for. I think he's planning on doing something. I know he is. He told me he was gonna have guys there. And I was to ignore them and do my job."

Desi frowned. "If he kicked your ass, how'd he think you'd be there tonight?"

And this was where it was going to get messy. "He told me a few days ago."

Realization dawned on Desi's face, and guilt clogged my throat.

"You were working Atlas?"

"I never wanted to, and I didn't tell Vick who the party was for, and that's why I'm in this bed. He found out, knew I lied, and said I no longer could be trusted."

Desi didn't say anything more. He took out his cell phone and stepped out of the room. I turned to face Poppy. There was no anger or disappointment in her gaze. There was understanding. She knew me better than anyone, and she knew I'd had no choice.

"It's going to be okay, Toby." She squeezed my hand.

"Atlas isn't going to want anything to do with me after he finds out."

She pressed another kiss to my hand. "Let him make up his own mind, brother."

I rested my head back, closed my eyes, and waited for whatever was to come.

CHAPTER TWENTY-THREE

Atlas

"I have a list of songs requested by Sam Ramos and his fiancé." Ledger handed me a clipboard. I wasn't completely focused; half my mind was elsewhere. I kept checking my cell phone every five minutes to see the words, "He's awake."

"Hey."

"Sorry, I'm trying to get my head in the game." I read over the list; all the songs seemed fine. "Looks good. I trust you, Ledger. Why'd you feel the need to show me?"

"To get you out of your head."

It was like someone was squeezing my heart. I wanted to be sitting right next to Toby and—

"You really fucking like this guy." Ledger broke through my thoughts. "It's about goddamn time you felt something for someone else. And it sucks a fuckload he's in a hospital bed beat to shit. You wanna be there." He wasn't asking me; he knew. "Look, get out of here. We still have like four hours before the guests of honor arrive. Max and I can order people around until then. Go see him."

He squeezed my shoulder, and my hand instinctively reached over and clung to it. "Thank you."

I rushed out the back to my car, and halfway to the hospital, my cell rang. I hit the button on my steering wheel, bringing the call to my car speaker. "Yeah?"

"Atlas?" It was Desi.

"You called me. Don't you know who you're talking to?"

He chuckled. "Sorry, sounds weird."

"You're on speaker, I'm in my car on the way to the hospital. I want to be there when he wakes up, and I have four hours. So hopefully I won't miss it."

"Yeah, so, you missed it. He's awake."

I couldn't even be mad. He was awake, and that was a good sign. "Good. I'll be there in a minute."

"Hold up."

I stopped at a red light and listened. He told me how Vick was planning something with my party, and while that nearly had me turning my car around to get back to the club, thinking I'd catch whoever it was, it was the next words out of his mouth that made me freeze up.

"Atlas, Toby has been working for Vick in more than a staff way."

"No."

"Listen. I'm not sure he was working for him voluntarily. People like Vick Keller, they don't give you many choices when it comes to doing things. He had to be holding something over Toby's head."

Horns blaring had me looking up. The light was green, but I didn't move. Cars whizzed around me beeping, hollering.

"Atlas. Vick caught him lying. He wouldn't give info on your party, but he knew already. Beat Toby for lying."

"Shit." The light was red again, so I took a second to calm down. I still wanted to see Toby, but I was messed up over this.

Familiar emotions of a time long ago surfaced. But Toby wasn't Joker. I knew that. I did.

"He doesn't know you're coming. Listen, Atlas, I have no idea what Vick is planning, but I don't think you throw a morsel like a senator's son at him and he ignores it."

When the light turned green, I moved this time. I made a U-turn, heading toward the club. "Tell Toby I will be there after the bachelor party. As angry as I am, I don't want him worrying. It won't be good for him."

"Okay. Keep me posted?"

"Yeah. How is he, Desi?"

"Shoulder's in a sling thing, concussion. No major damage to his eye, they think, but he got stitches and he has to heal. But he'll be okay."

"Good. Talk to you later." I hit the button, ending the call, and raced back to Joker's Sin. I had to figure out how to keep that party going but keep Vick out.

———

"What the fuck are you doing here?" Max asked as I entered the club.

I spent the next half hour explaining everything Desi told me and then came to a conclusion I wasn't sure was perfect, but it would have to do. I wouldn't have Vick making me run, but I could stop him from getting close.

"We're closing the club tonight, leaving it open just for the bachelor party. One thing Senator Ramos told me was that people invited to the bachelor party were mailed a special bracelet. So if they don't have that on, they don't get in. Aside from our security, they will have their own. I think we could get through the party easily without Vick getting near."

"Closing the club on a Friday?" Max asked as he rested his elbows on the bar top.

"No choice. I can't police the floor and the VIP area, and I don't have enough security to do both effectively. Without knowing what Vick is hoping to accomplish, I'd rather have a club to open Saturday than none at all."

They all nodded in agreement, and we got to work devising a plan. There were some patrons deemed regulars that I knew were good people. Ledger was tasked with inviting them to dance on the stage to keep things fun. I went to my office and sent a message to Sam Ramos explaining I would be closing the club instead of just the floor. To keep him from worrying, I simply said it was a gift from me to them.

By the time everything was done, there were a couple of hours until the party began. I checked in with Desi, and he said Toby was fine. Poppy was still there with him, and I explained what we were doing. He agreed that Poppy needed to stay where she was, knowing once Vick realized his plan wasn't going to work, he'd be livid. Then I went to the website and posted that the club was closed for a private party. With nothing left to do businesswise, I went to my bathroom, showered and changed, getting ready for the night. As I washed my body, my thoughts weren't consumed with the event about to take place; they were filled with what I'd say to Toby when I saw him later.

The irrational side of me wanted to rage and scream and ask why he couldn't come to me and tell me. The other calmer side realized he likely had no choice, and for that reason I'd hear him out before deciding my next steps.

I chose a gold-and-black suit, because one, it was fun and I looked amazing in it, and two, the party tonight was a true affair that was deserving of the best fashion. A little gold face powder, kohl around the eyes, and I was good to go.

Nothing was going to ruin this night. And when it was all over, I'd go down to the hospital and try to see if whatever Toby and I had going on was salvageable.

CHAPTER TWENTY-FOUR

Toby

Every time I woke, it felt like the nurse was giving me more medicine, and I was passing out again. I was glad to see Poppy was still there. In one of my more lucid moments, she explained that Desi told her she had to stay until he knew it was safe.

I wasn't sure how much Atlas knew or how much Desi told him, and I was trying not to misread the fact that he hadn't tried to communicate with me as personal. Desi said all he knew was that Atlas had a plan for the bachelor party, and I was hoping that meant everything would be okay.

"How are we doing this evening, Mr. St. Claire?" A doctor I'd seen a few times smiled and checked my vitals.

"Sore. I'd like to be able to stay awake a little longer than five minutes if possible."

He chuckled. And I noticed he had a nice smile, kind eyes. But I was also paranoid. I didn't know who to trust. Who Vick knew.

"I understand, but your body is in that 'need to heal' mode.

Physical therapy and such will follow soon enough, but the pain is there, and we need you as relaxed as possible." He moved to my shoulder, removing the ice pack. "Swelling has lessened. I can remove this for a bit, but if the swelling returns, it goes back."

It was better than nothing. There was no question it was freezing. "I'll take what I can get."

"Do you have any idea how long he'll be in the hospital?" Poppy asked as she moved closer to my bed.

"Tomorrow I'll run a few more scans and tests and give you a good time frame. I don't like to guess on anything." His blue eyes twinkled as he smiled at me. "Would you like more painkillers? I could give you some time without them, but I would ask that when you begin to hurt too much you call the nurse."

"If it's okay, I'd like to stay a little lucid."

He nodded and said he'd inform the nursing staff and see me tomorrow. After he left, I turned my head to where Desi was facing the window.

"Desi?"

He turned and came over to my bed. "Yeah?"

"Have you spoken to Atlas? Does he know…what I did?"

Desi had been pretty quiet. I knew he was a friend of Ciro's, and he was watching out for me. He didn't apologize, but I knew he felt bad something had happened to me. He wasn't a horrible guy, and right then he was my only link to Atlas.

"I told him. I can't tell you what he'll do, but he did say he'd come by after the party." He spoke with no inflection.

"That's gotta be good then, if he's coming by," Poppy said with a small smile.

"I don't expect Atlas to forgive me. I'd just like the chance to apologize to him."

Desi nodded and went back to the window. He wasn't a talker but oddly, it felt good having him around. I knew while my eyes were closed, he was watching over Poppy and keeping her safe.

For the next hour, the three of us were able to eat something, and we kept the TV on just in case there was some breaking news. Never in my life had I watched the news because I wanted updates on someone I knew.

After eating I was hurting pretty bad, so the nurse came in and gave me something. I wanted to be in better shape for Atlas when he came, so I thought it best to rest for a while. Both Desi and Poppy promised they'd wake me when he arrived and wouldn't let him leave until I got to apologize.

———

"Toby?" I heard Atlas's voice, and I wasn't sure if I was dreaming about the man. But then I kept hearing it and fought the strong drugs to open my eyes. He was slightly blurry, but there he was. He wore a black T-shirt and maybe jeans; I couldn't tell since he was sitting down and quite close to me.

"Atlas?"

He didn't give me his typical bright smile, but there was a twinge of happiness there when I said his name.

"I was just going to go, but your sister was adamant that I wake you." He looked over his shoulder to where I assumed Poppy was. "You really should rest, though. I can come back tomorrow."

"No." My good arm shot out and I grabbed his hand. "I need to talk to you."

His head dropped, and there was no hiding that Atlas had some battle going on inside that mind of his.

"Poppy and I will go to the waiting room, have a coffee, whatever. You two take your time," Desi said.

"Thank you," I said and waited until they left to face Atlas again.

"Before I say anything, can you tell me how the party went?"

He huffed out a laugh, but his attention was on me again, and damn, he was beautiful. "It went well, actually. Sam and Jeremy are ridiculously in love, and there was a lot of drinking, dancing, and zero issues. We closed the club minus the party, and between my security and the senator's, there was no way Vick or anyone was ruining the night."

"Did he try?"

"I had put on the website that the club was closed for a private affair, and some people didn't read it and tried to get in. If any of them were Vick's people, Ciro didn't say."

I tried to sit up, but pain shot through my shoulder.

"Stop. I'll hit the button so you can rise." He did so and watched intently as I attempted to get comfortable. I wasn't sure if I wanted to cry or beg for forgiveness.

"Thanks."

"Toby, I want to understand. I want to give you the benefit of the doubt." His hand touching mine was better than all the pain medicine. "Regardless of what you did to me, you didn't deserve what Vick did or has been doing to you."

"I never wanted to lie to you, Atlas. Ever. So many times I wanted to tell you what was happening, but every time I was face-to-face with Vick, he knew things. And he has someone shadowing Poppy. He promised if I even thought about saying a thing, he'd get to Poppy faster than anyone else would."

He nodded, his finger lazily tracing patterns over my hand. "I can see why that could be scary. But you could've talked to me in my office or written it down and slipped it to me. Told me why you were doing it."

"You mean I should've trusted you."

I hated the long silence. Atlas searched my face, and I didn't know what he wanted to hear.

"I'm sorry, Atlas."

"No. I get it. Why would you trust me? We kissed. We had a good time and—"

"Wait a sec. I know what you're about to do. I've heard this before. You're about to say it was good while it lasted, even though we never had anything, just the start of something that could've been amazing. You're gonna cut me loose, right?" I released a humorless laugh. "You'll promise to have people watch over me and Poppy, so nothing happens." He didn't say anything right away. "How close am I?"

"Toby, I get it. I totally understand why you did what you did. And I want to just say fuck it, water under the bridge, and move on. But I can't, I..." He sighed.

"Because someone did one hell of a number on you once upon a time, you're going to punish the world for it." His golden eyes met mine. "Now, how close am I?"

"Close."

CHAPTER TWENTY-FIVE

Atlas

Staring at Toby's bruised face, seeing the pain he'd endured to right his wrongs, to save his sister, made me want to blurt it all out. Tell him everything about Joker so maybe he'd understand why I couldn't be in a relationship built on lies. And why was I saying "relationship"? *Because a part of you wants that again, but this time with someone who won't break every part of who you are.*

"Atlas, you have no reason to trust me. I won't even ask you to. But just know, if I had a choice, I would've never done this. If I thought I could have packed up me and Poppy and ran, I would've."

I didn't want him to run away. "Toby, listen to me." I inched closer and this time instead of just lightly touching his fingers, I took his hand in mine.

"I want to tell you, explain myself. It's weird—I've never wanted that. I told Ciro, Max, and Ledger, they saw what that life with Joker did to me."

"Tell me if you want, but I'll never ask."

"I know. I appreciate that." I could see cuts on his hand. I moved my inspection up his arm to his face, shattered. His shoulder was immobile, his breathing was okay, but I could tell it was hurting for him to take each breath. He didn't need me walking away from him right then. He needed people who were going to help him, and if nothing more ever happened with Toby and me, it would be okay because he'd be safe.

"How about we lighten things up a little. Tell me more about the party tonight." He lifted one side of his mouth, which normally would be adorable, but any movement just looked painful on him.

"Sure." I sat with him for another half hour, telling him everything. From the drinks to the cake. How Sparkles was there and started everyone on a dance-off and how Sam and Jeremy were ridiculously in love. He smiled, and I noticed his blinks getting longer. And by the time I was done, he was asleep.

"He fell asleep on you, huh?" I hadn't heard the door open so when Poppy spoke, I jumped. "Sorry, didn't mean to startle you."

"It's fine."

She looked over at her brother and then to me. "I hated him working for Vick. I'd tell him all the time to quit, but he wouldn't. We needed the money. My job just doesn't pay enough. For the most part, he just worked and came home. Vick never bothered him. But one day, that changed."

"The day Vick confronted him?"

She nodded. "Desi actually explained a lot more to me than Toby ever did, but Toby's always been quite protective of me." She appeared amused, not angry with her brother. "Desi told me how Vick threatened me. Had someone following me around. Of course Toby was going to do anything for me he could."

She met my eyes, sharp, assessing. "Toby and I only have each other. It's been just the two of us for a while. And yeah, Toby has always been enamored by you. *The Atlas Durand.* But you were like a dream for him, something out of reach. He never wanted to hurt you or your club, but he was backed into a corner. Please, don't be angry with him."

I'd loosened my grip on Toby's hand after he'd fallen asleep, but our fingers were still wrapped together, entwined. I stared at them, at the contrast of our skin. It was beautiful and we fit. Perfectly.

"You're a good sister, Poppy. And yeah, I was mad at Toby, but I do understand. It's just not easy for me to forget and trust."

"I hope you work it out." She wheeled over to the other side of the bed and placed her hand on her brother's knee.

"Work it out with Toby?" I shrugged. "I don't know."

"No. I didn't mean my brother; I mean yeah, that would be ideal, but I meant work it out with you. You're all jigsaw pieces with no picture."

She was right. I was a mess. I loved my life, my club, my friends. But when it came to my love life, it was endless fucks and no sustainability, and I knew why.

"I'm going to head home and get some rest. Tell Toby I'll come back in the morning."

"You will?" She smiled so brightly, it was contagious.

"Yeah."

As I left, Desi said he'd stay the night in the room with Toby and Poppy, and I told him when I returned in the morning, he could take a break for a few hours.

When I pulled into the parking garage of my building, the exhaustion of the evening began to really slam into me. In the elevator up to my floor, I rested my head against the wall the whole time. The doors opened and when I stepped onto my floor, George, one of the building's security guys, was there.

"Good evening, Mr. Durand. I'm sorry to bother you so late. You had a visitor this evening, but because you weren't here and they weren't on the list of people, I didn't let him up. He was a little belligerent, but when I agreed to at least let him leave you a note, he was okay with that." He handed me a piece of paper.

"Who was the guy?"

I opened the note. At the same time George said, "Vick Keller."

I'm done playing games, was all the note said.

"I didn't think you associated with Mr. Keller," George said.

"I don't." I crumpled the note in my fist and met George's eyes. "And don't be respectful of the man; he hasn't earned that. Next time he comes here, if he comes here, call the police. He's not welcome."

"Understood."

I went into my place, the lights turning on automatically, and I immediately called Ciro. Told him everything going on and he said we really needed to figure out how we were going to handle this.

"He has police on his payroll. Any idea which officers they might be?"

"No," he said. "But I happen to know a detective I can trust who would likely have a good idea."

"Give 'em a call and see if they'd be willing to help us."

"Will do. Stay safe, Atlas."

"You too."

When someone like Vick Keller said he was done playing games, and you didn't even know you were playing one, that was something to take seriously. He didn't get offended and slap your hand. He got angry and destroyed your life.

There was nothing more I could do tonight, so I took a quick shower, threw on some silk pajama pants, and lay in bed. I stared at the ceiling for hours, replaying everything Toby said, the note Vick left, and when I finally fell asleep, I dreamed of all the heartache Joker had tattooed onto my heart.

CHAPTER TWENTY-SIX

Toby

One thing about hospitals was, they started their mornings way too early—like advanced morning. The doctor from yesterday walked in while the sky was just brightening. He was smiling and chipper and clearly Satan.

"Good morning, Mr. St. Claire." He went right over to my machines, smiling at my sister and Desi. His jacket said his name, which I kept forgetting.

"Good morning, Dr. Toth."

"You remembered my name." He was so happy, and I hated to burst his bubble but…

"No. I can read." I pointed to his jacket.

"Ah, clearly you're feeling better." He read over a few things before speaking. "The night nurse said you had a quiet night. Everything is looking good. We want to run some tests today, as you know. Nurse Shell here will take your blood, and after some breakfast, we can get those scans in. Sound all right?"

"Thrilling."

Nurse Shell came over and took blood, a lot of vials of it, and said she was off to get my breakfast.

"Atlas will be here this morning. Once he arrives, Desi and I will go get a bite."

"Actually, I'll be heading out for a few hours after Atlas gets here. He said he'd stay a while, so I'm gonna go do some things."

Maybe it was my imagination, but Poppy looked crestfallen. "Are you coming back?" she asked.

His smile was small, but his cheeks pinked and… *Oh, no way!*

"Yes, this afternoon."

Poppy seemed happier with that. "Can I ask you to stop at our apartment and get me some clothes and a few things?"

He nodded, and she grabbed a piece of paper and wrote down a list. "Need anything, Toby?"

"Maybe my cell phone. I left it at Vick's, but Poppy said Shane brought it over and left it in our mailbox. Charger too, that's in my nightstand."

"Okay." He took the list and shoved it into his pocket.

My breakfast came, and still Atlas hadn't arrived. "Look, why don't you two just go. Nothing is happening to me here. I can't eat while you two stare at me."

Desi and Poppy met each other's eyes. Had some stupid silent conversation, then nodded. "Okay, we'll go get food and come back up here to eat it," Desi said. "It's the best you get."

"Oh, ten whole minutes of alone time?" I joked, earning myself the finger from Desi.

After they left, I ate as quickly as I could. It was oatmeal, fruit, and tea, easy things I only needed one hand for. The food was okay, but I wanted to go home so badly. I'd just finished my oatmeal when the door opened, and a police officer entered.

"Mr. St. Claire?" he said.

"Hi, yes." I knew they were likely going to be coming to talk to me, so it had been just a matter of time.

"I'm Officer Milne. I wanted to speak with you about what happened to put you in that bed there." He smiled, seemingly harmless. Cops in Haven Hart weren't revered. Too much corruption so I knew right off the bat I would be giving him the bare minimum.

"Oh, I don't think I'll be much help, Officer."

"And why's that?" He stood next to my bed, eyes narrowed.

"I was mugged. Guy, or guys maybe, came up behind me. Took my things and kept hitting me. I didn't see anything."

"Hmm. You're sure? Maybe something one of them said or maybe how they smelled?"

I shook my head slowly as there was a throb lingering, so moving it was painful. "No. I remember getting up and being just a block from home. When I got there, my sister saw me and called the police and ambulance."

Officer Milne leaned down then, very close to my face. "It's probably best you remember it that way." And this was why no one trusted the cops in Haven Hart. The bad outweighed the good by too much.

"Yeah."

"Is there a problem here, Officer?" Atlas's voice had the cop moving away from the bed and turning. Relief washed over me when I saw him standing by the door. Dressed in jeans and a white shirt, he looked just as amazing as he did when he wore his fancy clothes.

"Mr. Durand. No, I was just asking Mr. St. Claire about the night he was mugged."

"Mugged?" Atlas said, eyes moving from me back to the cop.

"That's right. Mugged." He said the last word slowly.

"I see." Atlas walked fully into the room and came over to the other side of my bed. "Well, if you have everything, I think it's best you go."

"I'm the police officer here, Mr. Durand. I'll decide when I go."

Atlas shrugged, fearless in the face of corruption. "So, if I paid you five hundred bucks right now to get the fuck out of this hospital room, you wouldn't go?" He pulled out his wallet, and the cop eyed it. "Isn't that how you roll, Officer?"

When the door opened again, my sister and Desi came in, and now the officer took a few steps back.

"I have all I need here, I'll just be going." He made a hasty retreat and once he was gone, it was as if we all released one collective breath.

"Where were you?" Atlas asked Desi.

"I told them to go get breakfast. I didn't think anything would happen, and it didn't. That cop wasn't going to touch me—he was likely sent by Vick to see if I was talking."

"I don't need to be at the club until five, Desi. Why don't you get out of here, relax or whatever." Atlas grabbed a chair and pulled it up to my bed.

"He has scans soon," Desi said as he chomped on some toast. "I'll go after I eat and…" He looked at me, then Poppy. "Maybe Poppy, if you want, you can come with me? Get you out of here for a little?"

"Is that safe?" I asked.

"I won't leave her side." Desi smiled.

"Not to be negative or anything, but two times now, Toby's been in danger when you were supposed to be watching him." Atlas sat back, glaring at Desi.

"And you think I'll let someone hurt Poppy or you think I'm incompetent?"

Poppy and I smiled and rolled our eyes. "Guys, shut up. I would love to go with Desi. Hospitals are exhausting, and I'd rather get all those things on that list myself."

So, after they finished eating, they both said good-bye, and then Atlas and I were alone.

"It seems we have hours with each other," I said, sipping my now-cold tea. "What do you want to do?"

He cocked his head, his expression unreadable. "We're gonna talk in between the doctors sticking you with things and scanning you."

"Talk about what?"

He huffed, and I knew whatever it was, it was hard for him. "I think I'm gonna tell you why I'm all jigsaw pieces inside my head."

I laughed the second he said that. "Sweet lord, you've been talking to Poppy, haven't you?"

This made him echo my laughter and nod. "The girl is scary."

"That she is." I waved my hand toward him. "The floor is yours. Say whatever it is you want to tell me."

CHAPTER TWENTY-SEVEN

Atlas

"I was Joker's sin. Literally. I spent so much time thinking if it wasn't for me, he'd still be here, and we'd still be tearing shit up." I closed my eyes and like always, his face appeared behind my lids…the last time I ever saw him.

"We were young and stupid, mostly. But we were okay. My mom wasn't the greatest mother and like so many kids, I was tossed into the system when I was fifteen, thinking that was a better choice. I met Joker there."

Toby squeezed my hand and I opened my eyes, keeping them downcast and focused on our fingers.

"We ran away on my seventeenth birthday. He was a year younger, and we'd had enough of the crappy foster homes and beatings we didn't deserve. Social workers didn't give a shit, so we had to do something ourselves. It was street life for us for a long time. Drugs, sex, a lot I'm not proud of, but we did what we had to do to survive, and one night we got lucky.…Well, we thought we did. This guy, Sal, in a stupid fancy car asked us if we wanted to go to a party. It was fucking cold that night, and the thought of being warm was everything. So we said yes. That of course, came with a price, and the next thing we knew, we were running cons and scams for him. Anything he asked for, we did it."

I could hear carts rolling by out in the hall, nurses and doctors chattering, but it was quiet in Toby's room, and he was simply listening. I never thought getting this off my chest to him would feel so good.

"That was the beginning of the end for us. Parties melded together. We were swimming in cash after a year. It was like we traded one drug for another. Joker was always so charismatic and funny, he was pulling in twice as much as I was. He was also getting hooked on coke and whatever else he could get his hands on." Toby gave my fingers another squeeze.

"We had this place where we were living, and one night he overdosed. But I got him to the hospital, and he went into rehab and yeah, for years we had a life. We were able to get away from that cesspool, and we did real work. Made honest money. We still had all the money we'd earned doing all that shit, but we wanted to hold on to it." Shaking my head, I remembered how bad it had gotten at one point.

"Then Joker came home one day, said he was promoted. I was happy and it was great, and suddenly he was bringing in three times his regular money. He was also getting distant, and I knew something was up.

"I was with him for twelve years before it all went to shit. Can you imagine loving someone that long, only to have it all end with one bad choice?"

I met Toby's eyes, and they glistened with tears; he knew this wasn't going to end well. "That's hard, Atlas."

Nodding, I went on, this time without looking away. "I told him I knew something was up and told him to tell me what it was. We fought. God, how we fought. But he told me he ran into that guy who saved us all those years ago at a bar, Sal. He'd been working with him. See, Joker worked at the airport, so he was fudging shit so this guy could get his drugs into Haven Hart."

"Jesus."

"Yeah. One night he was supposed to meet a plane on the tarmac at a certain time, but it was my birthday. I told him if he went, I wouldn't be here when he got back. I was done. I couldn't live like that anymore." His face was in every blink. His blue eyes filled with worry, fear, and resolution. "I think he knew staying with me would kill him, but he never said anything. He just stayed. In that moment, I was just glad he was with me. I didn't think anything horrible would happen with missing one night."

"He loved you," Toby whispered.

"Yeah, well, the next day there was a raid on a couple of hangars at the airport. A shit-ton of drugs were seized, and Joker was to blame because he wasn't there to shuffle shit around."

"Oh, no."

"Yeah. We were watching the news on our couch, in our fucking house, when the knock came. Not the cops like you'd think. No. Him. Sal had four guys with him, and they held Joker down. I—" I was talking so fast, I ran out of air and gasped.

"Breathe, Atlas, please." A lone tear slid along his cheek, and I knew he was feeling everything I was. The horror, pain, the embedded sadness that choked me in the middle of the night. The reason I never wanted to love again.

"I sat there as they beat him, and when I'd yell at them to stop, I'd get the same treatment. And when our tormentor kneeled in front of me, I begged him. Begged Sal to let us just run away. Said I'd give him everything we had if he let Joker live." I shook my head, hearing his laughter in my mind like an earworm. No matter how hard I tried, I always heard it.

"He told me I was Joker's sin. Joker stayed that night when he had other commitments and knew it. Staying with me was his sin, and for that he had to pay. Sal then…" I hiccupped, the emotion clogging my throat, my pulse throbbing in my ears, but I had to finish, I needed to. "He went over to Joker, took out a knife, and held it to his throat. He asked Joker if he had anything to say and he…" This time a sob wracked my body, I pressed my face against Toby's hand, and I cried.

"I'm here. It's okay, Atlas, I'm right here."

"Joker looked right at me, smiled, and said, 'I regret nothing and will love you forever.' And then I watched as he bled out on the floor in my living room. I watched until I blacked out."

Toby was quiet as I cried on his hand in his hospital room. When I lifted my head, I knew he had cried right along with me.

"I'm sorry, Atlas. My lying, it brought all this to the forefront for you."

I shook my head. "No, that's the thing, Toby. It's always there. Every day. For the last ten years."

"Oh, Atlas. You've held on to all that guilt for a decade?"

I didn't answer that, just continued talking. "A few years after Joker died, using all our money, I bought this plot and started to build the club. Yeah, I needed some investors, and I made some shitty choices. But it's all mine now, and I owe nobody anything."

I could see in Toby's gaze his need for forgiveness and how badly I wanted to give it to him.

"Your lies were nothing like what Joker did, Toby. I get that, maybe not in the moment when Desi told me everything, but why you did it? The motivation. I get it. You never did it to hurt anyone, you did it to save everyone."

"Thank you," Toby said so quietly, had I not been right there, I probably would've missed it. We were silent for a moment before Toby spoke again.

"Can I ask what happened to that guy Sal?" I knew he'd want to know.

"It's Haven Hart, Toby." I smiled. "He pissed off a mob boss and he was wiped out."

He nodded in understanding. "So you named the place after something a dead piece of shit called you the night he murdered the love of your life?"

Chuckling, I said, "Ciro, Max, and Ledger all said the same thing. But yeah. It's a reminder."

"To what? Not love anyone?"

"No, Toby, it's a reminder that love truly is the most powerful thing out there. It's also the most dangerous."

He cocked his head, his lips quirked. "Power and love aren't always bad, Atlas."

I never got to respond to that because a nurse came in a second later, saying Toby had to have scans. I was able to follow and stand outside the testing room. When we entered Toby's room a couple of hours later, we were both starving.

The doctor said it would be okay if I ordered something from the diner since Toby wasn't on any dietary restrictions. So, for the rest of the afternoon we sat, ate, and kept the conversation light. We'd both had enough heavy for one day. Something told me things were going to get worse before they got better.

CHAPTER TWENTY-EIGHT

Toby

Desi and Poppy returned shortly after four, and the doctor came to talk with us before Atlas had to leave.

"Good news, Toby. You can be released Monday." The doctor addressed the rest of the room. "I'll keep him here another day to have a physical therapist come by to speak with Toby. He needs to keep the sling on for a while longer, but there are things he can do. He will need to schedule PT, though. The scans showed no bleeds or anything of great concern. The stitches are dissolvable, so let them do their thing. However, he needs to take it easy for at least a week or two."

"I need to work." It was a response born from instinct, thinking I had to work. For all I knew, I didn't have a job anymore.

"I'm his boss, he's fine. Go on, Doc." He shot me a glare I wanted to return, but he wasn't firing me. I still had a job.

"Right," the doctor continued, "he will need help, likely showering and such until he can comfortably do it on his own. We don't realize how much we rely on two arms and hands until one isn't there."

"Well, I can help some," Poppy said but I knew she couldn't, and she wasn't going to want to see her brother naked. And lord knew, I didn't want her to see me naked.

"Not to worry, Doc. We'll figure it all out. He can stay with me for a week or so until he gets his groove back."

I sputtered, Poppy laughed, and the doc…well, he was happy with that. I decided to wait until he was out of the room to stand my ground on this.

"I'm not leaving Poppy alone. In case you forgot, Atlas, Vick's crazy and probably wants to kill us both."

"I know. Vick sent me a note that he was done playing games." Atlas leaned over my bed, an inch from my face. "I'm not playing with him, Toby."

"Why are you just telling me this now?"

"I'm a big girl, Toby," Poppy interrupted Atlas's and my conversation.

"I'll stay with her," Desi said, and what the fuck was going on?

"Perfect. Desi's got Poppy. I do think it's safer she not stay at their place, though." I listened as Atlas, Desi, and Poppy came up with a temporary plan until they knew how to deal with Vick. My mind was still reeling over Vick's threats.

"I'll be back in the morning. I'm not working, so I can stay the night here, and then Monday, I'll take Toby to my place."

"Do I get any say in this?"

"Not really," Poppy said at the same time Atlas and Desi said no. And a part of me wanted to argue, but a bigger part felt cared for, safe…safer than I'd felt in a long time. So I relented.

"Fine."

Atlas kissed the top of my head and left. Poppy was smiling, and Desi chuckled.

"I knew you two would be okay," she said as she turned the TV on and settled in.

———

THE FOLLOWING MORNING, after a restless sleep brought on by worry over Poppy's safety and dreams about what Atlas had gone through with Joker, Atlas arrived with Ciro and a woman I didn't recognize. Poppy and Desi said they'd go get breakfast, seeing as the room was really crowded now.

"Morning," Atlas said and kissed my forehead. "This is Tracey Wilding; she's a detective with the Haven Hart Police Department."

"Call me TJ," she said, extending her hand. I shook it with my good hand but eyed Ciro and Atlas. Were they serious? They wanted me to talk to the police? Tracey, or TJ as she preferred, laughed. "The look on your face is priceless, Toby."

"I've known TJ for a real long time, Toby," Ciro said. "She's one of the good ones; she may be able to help us."

She had a kind smile, her brown hair with wine-colored tints was up in a ponytail, and her dark, squared glasses shimmered under the light. She was wearing jeans and a sweat shirt, so I was under the impression she wasn't on official police business.

"I know an Officer Milne came to see you yesterday," she said, to which I nodded. "Yeah, he's got questionable morals and no loyalty. All you'd have to do is outbid whoever's paying him, and he'd be yours."

"If there are so many corrupt cops, why doesn't anyone do anything about it?" I asked the obvious question.

"When corruption goes all the way to the top, it's not easy." Her expression was somber.

"Why do you stay?"

She shrugged at my question. "I guess I've always been one of those people who believes one person can make a difference."

"So tell us, TJ, what do you think you can do to help us if so many above you are gonna do everything in their power to dismantle any justice you try to uphold?" Atlas asked as he sat in the chair beside my bed.

"That's the thing, Atlas—we have a lot of corrupt cops, but they don't all work for the same asshole."

Ciro chuckled, and I knew I was missing something.

"I can go to Vick's, arrest him and Liberio, hold them for maybe twenty-four hours, but they'll get out and be quite pissed."

"Twenty-four hours could be enough time. A lot happens in a day." I believed what Atlas was saying.

"Agreed, but in that twenty-four hours, we need to have a solid plan so that when Vick Keller is released, he's walking out with no help and no army."

"So what do you recommend, TJ?" Ciro asked, but the light in his eyes told me he knew.

"Aside from me believing that one person can change things, I also believe the line in the movie *Demolition Man*." She grinned, and I was trying to remember what line she was referring to.

"The line about licking meat?" Atlas asked, and we all laughed.

"No," TJ said. "We send a maniac to catch a maniac."

"You know of such a maniac?" I was worried this may get out of hand.

It was Atlas who answered. He took my hand, and I looked over at him. "That guy, the one who killed Joker, remember how I told you what happened to him?"

"Yeah."

"He pissed off someone bigger than him."

Oh. "You want to get some big bad guy to take care of Vick for us?" He nodded. "Who?"

"That's what I'm going to find out," TJ answered. "I'm going to do some digging. See what Vick is into and maybe work out what district and who may help us without even realizing it."

"What do we do in the meantime?" I asked.

"You'll rest today, and tomorrow I'll take you to my place, where you'll heal and hopefully when you're able to function better, TJ will have some answers."

"That's a good plan," she said. "I'll be in touch with Ciro. You all stay safe." She said good-bye and left with Ciro.

"What do I do while you're working?" It would mean I'd be left alone at his place.

"I spoke with the security of my building. No one is getting up to my penthouse. I'll be with you until about five every night and be back right after closing. You're not incapable, you just need some help. It'll be fine, we can work it out."

He seemed so confident, I had no reason to burst his bubble, so I said okay and left it at that. I had no doubt I was going to go stir-crazy.

CHAPTER TWENTY-NINE

Atlas

I paid my cleaning service to come by Sunday evening to really clean my place and change all the sheets. I explained to them that I was going to be having a guest, so they promised to clean from top to bottom in the guest room. I also made sure the fridge and cabinets were filled, so there was plenty of food. I couldn't believe how nervous I was to have Toby staying with me.

By the time he was discharged Monday morning, Toby was antsy. He got upset when they wouldn't let him walk out of there, and he had to get wheeled out. His sister saying at least he could get out of it shut him up real fast.

Desi was renting a small place on the outskirts of Haven Hart where he'd keep Poppy protected, and Ciro would do apartment runs when it was needed. Keeping the St. Claire twins safe was our top priority.

"Wow, you live here?" Toby said as he slowly made his way into the penthouse. It was an overcast day, so the windows painted a picture of gloom over an unscrupulous city.

"Yeah. I bought it after I opened Joker's Sin. I wanted to be above it all." It was true, and the vulnerable feeling, being so exposed to Toby, was hard for me.

"It's gorgeous, Atlas." Toby moved over to one of the windows and laughed. "It's so scary and exhilarating."

"That's exactly how I felt the first time I stood there too." I let him take it all in for a few minutes. "Let me show you to your room." He followed behind me, and I placed a couple of his bags on the bed.

"This room is the size of my entire apartment." He scanned his surroundings in wonderment.

The walls were slate gray with white trim and a speckled black, white, and gray carpet. The windows were floor-to-ceiling like the rest of the penthouse. It was a king-sized bed with a gray-and-black comforter. The en suite, which Toby was walking into currently, had a Jacuzzi tub, a shower stall, and a toilet. But it was spacious.

"Do you like it?" I asked as he stepped back into the room.

"It's beautiful. Thanks for doing this, Atlas."

I moved over to Toby, crowding him slightly. The scent of hospital was strong on him, and I knew he probably wanted to clean up. But I had to say something.

"Please don't thank me. None of this should've ever happened to you or to me. But it has. I've faced some shit here in Haven Hart. I could tell you more stories. And I've thought of leaving so many times. But I built this and if one day I leave, it'll be my choice. I won't have anyone like Vick Keller pushing me out."

"I'd love to hear those stories," he said with a coy expression.

"And maybe if you're good, I'll tell you one."

"Oh?" He raised a brow.

"You need a bath, so that means you'll need my help." I was sure getting naked in front of me wasn't on the top of things he wanted to do today and if he did, not like this.

"Are you trying to get me naked?" Toby was flirting.

If he wasn't all banged up, I'd lift him, press him against the wall, and kiss him breathless. As it was, I needed to be tender with him.

"I very well might be." I winked and walked into the bathroom. Opening the drawer by the sink, I took out a few different bubble baths. "What's your favorite?"

He smirked and examined each one. "Oh, this looks good." He popped the top with his thumb and sniffed. "Sandalwood and vanilla?" None of them had names since I bought them at the farmers market. Just the logo of the husband-wife duo who made them.

"Very good."

He handed it to me, and I moved to the tub, making sure the water was hot but not scorching. I poured a little of the bubbles in and when I was happy with the amount, I turned around. Toby had managed to get his sweat pants off but was having trouble with the shirt.

"Let me help. We have to take the sling off to get the shirt off, then get it back on." As carefully as possible, I removed the sling. Toby held his arm close to his body. I knew there was no way I was going to be able to get this shirt off without hurting him.

"Is this a favorite shirt of yours?"

"No…why?" He furrowed his brows.

"Like if I spilled bleach on it while doing laundry, would you be mad?"

"Are you telling me you're bad at doing laundry?" He chuckled.

"No, um. Just…" I took the collar in both hands and tore at it until it was ripped open.

"Oh. That's why you were asking. Yeah, it's okay if you rip my shirt off…oh never mind, you already did." I could tell by his expression he wasn't mad.

"I'll make sure Ciro brings button-down shirts."

"Probably wise."

When he was just in his boxers and socks, I took a moment to look at him. I hadn't really seen the rest of his body but as I took it in, I saw the bruises. How much of his skin was black and blue, yellow and purple.

"Hey." Toby, still holding his bad arm close, reached out, and placed his other hand on my arm. "I'm okay. I am."

"I can't wait until Vick pays." I could hear the growl in my voice, but it didn't frighten Toby; he grinned.

"Well, tiger, can I bathe first?"

Realizing he was holding his injured arm, I grabbed the sling and helped get it back on. I leaned down and removed his socks.

"I'm going to remove your boxers now."

"Yeah," his voice cracked. "Good idea."

I tried to give him dignity as I divested him of his boxers. But there was no way to ignore his erection when it sprang up and was an inch from my face.

"Well, damn," I whispered.

"You have that effect on it," Toby said, and I chuckled.

"Let's get you both washed up." My cock was trying to break free from the confines of my jeans, and as much as I wanted to take him in my mouth and taste him, I wouldn't take advantage of him.

I helped him into the tub. "Oh, hold on, I have an idea," I said and rushed into the kitchen. I grabbed a plastic bag.

"What's that?"

Carefully I tucked his arm and sling in the bag "Just in case, so the sling won't get wet."

He smiled. "That's genius."

Toby rested his head back and closed his eyes. I was about to leave when he spoke. "Aren't you going to wash me?" He never opened his eyes, but he wore a playful smirk.

"I suppose I can do that."

I grabbed a washcloth, squirted some body wash on it, got it all soapy, and started with his good shoulder and arm.

"Before you get out, we'll wash your hair."

"Sounds like a plan."

I was doing just fine, trying not to think about how his body felt as I washed him. Then I reached his cock and he hummed. *Fuck.*

CHAPTER THIRTY

Toby

The second Atlas brought the washcloth to my very hard cock, I couldn't stop the sound from leaving me. Even though I was sore—I ached in all the wrong places—and my arm was in a sling, I wanted him. I wanted him so fucking bad.

"It's going to be weird jacking myself later with my other hand…never did that before."

"Shit," Atlas whispered and damn, it felt good to see him so flustered.

"Unless, maybe…" I didn't know when it was that I became so bold. The man used to terrify me in the best way; he was almost godly and unapproachable. But here, like this, going through all this shit, I saw that he was human. He was gorgeous and took my breath away, but he was carrying a past that weighed on him. He forgave me, and damn, if the lust-filled gaze he shot my way said anything, he wanted me too.

"Maybe…" He plopped the washcloth onto the floor, I didn't break eye contact. "I can't have you hurting yourself," he said, and then I felt his hand grip my cock.

"Holy fuck." I almost shot from his touch alone.

"So responsive." He hummed as he moved his fist up and down my shaft, agonizingly slow. "Damn, Toby, you're so hard."

"Shit, shit, shit." Apparently, I couldn't word. Wording wasn't a thing I did anymore.

"Gonna come for me?" He reached up, and when he pinched my nipple, I tried not to jolt my leg and splash water everywhere.

"Shit, Atlas, fuck."

"You okay?" He stopped moving his hand, concern adorning his face.

"Yes, please don't stop."

The deep chuckle sounded dirty and perfect and yes, he started jacking me faster. With my good hand, I gripped the tub; I wanted it to last and needed it to end. Shit, just him touching me was electrifying my entire body. I could feel him in my toes, my hair. Mother of all things…

"Oh, God, yes, yes."

"Yeah, come on, Toby, come for me, let me see you come apart."

His words, his feel, his smell, it was too much. A kaleidoscope of colors burst behind my lids as the most powerful orgasm ripped through me. My pulse throbbed in my ears, my toes curled, and fucking Christ, I was gasping for air.

"Now that's gorgeous," I heard Atlas say, and when I opened my eyes, he was right in front of me. I never got to speak before his mouth was on mine, kissing and licking. If he didn't stop, I'd be hard again in no time.

It felt like forever and yet mere seconds when he pulled away. "Let's wash that beautiful hair of yours now." I'd agree to anything he asked me right then, and since I still couldn't seem to word, I nodded.

He started draining the water and grabbed the sprayer that rested on the side of the tub. "Sit up and look up." Holding my arm close, I did as I was told, and warm water cascaded over my hair.

As he lathered my hair in shampoo and then conditioner, I moaned. His fingers felt amazing. Once again, he told me to put my head back, and water washed away everything.

"Let's get you dry." He smiled as he helped me out, and I noticed a very prominent bulge in his jeans.

"I'd really love to help with this." I cupped his erection, loving when he hissed.

"We have time, Toby." I was about to argue, but he started kissing me again, my wet body pressed against his dry, clothed one.

"If you don't get clothes on me soon, I will drop to my knees, suck you dry, and probably injure myself further…though that's a chance I'll happily take." He mirrored my happiness but shook his head.

"I want the sexy part, not the Toby breaking part. Let's get you a little better, and then I'd very much love to see you on your knees and my cock down your throat."

And there went all my words again.

———

I WAS BORED. Which was ridiculous since before Atlas left to go to the club, he showed me all the streaming channels, showed me the numbers to order food if I wanted to, and George the security guy would bring it up. He even let me use his kindle and said he had Kindle Unlimited to read what I wanted. *Why am I bored?*

I texted Poppy, who said she was good but had to go because she and Desi were going to watch a movie. I was one hundred percent convinced something was going on with those two, which actually made me happy. Many men in Poppy's life could never look beyond her wheelchair; Desi didn't seem to let it get in his way.

I texted Shane, who only got out one text saying shit was weird at Vick's, and he'd call me later. I was glad he was okay, and Vick was leaving him alone. I had to see if there was a way to get Shane into Joker's Sin, but maybe taking him away now would make it too dangerous. Then we'd have to watch someone else on top of keeping all of us safe.

I put on *Orange Is The New Black*, having never watched it, played some games on my phone, and at some point must've fallen asleep. I heard someone in the apartment, and it jolted me awake. I grabbed some weird artsy thing on the nightstand for a weapon and moved toward the living room.

I stepped out of my room; the lights were dim, and the noise was now in the kitchen. I had this odd sculpture that was heavy, cradled in my good arm, and my other in a sling. What did I think I was going to do here?

To calm my nerves, I took a deep breath, and I jumped into the kitchen with a roar, hoping to scare whoever broke in.

"Fucking hell!" Atlas shouted as he turned to glare at me. "What the fuck, Toby?"

"Oh, shit! I'm sorry, Atlas. I thought someone was breaking in."

He rolled his eyes, but at least he smiled. "Why are you cradling my *Frozen in Time* statue?"

I peered down at the sculpture, and yeah, it was a clocklike thing that appeared to be frozen.

"I was going to hit you over the head with it."

He chuckled and took the heavy sculpture from my arm. "That would do it. But I told you, no one can get in here, so it could only be me."

I followed him to the guest room, where he put the weird statue back. I then realized he actually had a lot of art.

"You like art?"

He shrugged. "I like supporting local business. Raven Poe Edgars is a local artist, and I've been to a few of his shows and like his stuff."

I just nodded. I didn't know much about art, so I didn't say anything about it. "What time is it?"

"Three in the morning. I just got home from work."

"Oh, I must've fallen asleep."

He came up to me, gently placing his hands on my arms. "Which is what you should've been doing."

He had circles under his eyes and weariness in his smile. "Rough night?"

"A little. Vick tried to get some of his guys in the club. He got a couple in, but they were easy to spot, and we had to get them out." He sighed, his breath fanning over my face.

"I'm sorry."

He kissed the tip of my nose and stepped away. "Once we hear from TJ, it'll make everything easier. We'll know better how to navigate all this."

"Okay. Why don't you go to bed? We can talk more later."

So tenderly he brushed his hand over my cheek, said good night, and left the room. I waited until I heard the door to his room close and then slipped into bed again. Sleep eluded me as I rested in the too-big, too-lonely bed, staring out the window where Haven Hart glittered with lights. I couldn't hear the place, but I didn't have to. Living here as long as I had, it thrummed through my veins. The way the wind sounded between the buildings, vendors shouting, laughter, and conversations. The day always sounded different from the night. Where children's joy morphed into grown people screaming. Haven Hart was the best and the worst of humanity.

I watched the sun rise and marveled at how innocent the morning light made the city look. It was a new day.

CHAPTER THIRTY-ONE

Atlas

Tuesday night at Joker's Sin was electric. We'd been advertising the Wet and Wild Wednesday that was going to be happening there the following night, so it'd been bringing people in since. Not sure what they expected would happen before it, but business was business. Fortunately there were no incidents with Vick's guys and when closing time came, Ledger, Max, Ciro, and I all sat at the bar, having a drink and talking about tomorrow.

"So, the temporary panels will come up around the stage to hold the water in and stop it from falling off the stage. We have dancers, and the plan is to do a wet bodysuit competition. Patrons will all vote who wins. The wetter they get, the harder it'll be to dance." Ledger chuckled. "I'll be behind a clear panel too. Gotta keep the equipment dry."

"And what's the dancer getting again?" Max asked.

"We were originally going to do a night out with Atlas, but with his new houseguest and all that possible murdering happening, we are offering the dancer who wins a two-hundred-dollar gift certificate to Vayne's and free drinks for a month."

"How nice of me," I said, and they all laughed.

"The guys set up the sprinklers above the stage, and the barrels are hooked up. Ledger just has to hit the switch," Ciro said.

"Sounds great. I'll be here a little earlier tomorrow to see. We should test it." I finished my drink in one gulp.

"We tested the sprinkler system already, but the barrels only hold enough for one dance, so I don't want to waste it. Plus if we get the whole stage soaked right before the show, it'll take too long to clean up in time for the event." Ledger said.

"If you're sure they work, that's good enough for me." Hopping off the stool, I said good night and told them I'd see them tomorrow.

"Hey, Atlas." Max slapped my arm and followed me to my car. "You should bring Toby. I know he can't work, but you could put him in the VIP area, give him his own section. He won't want to miss the show. This is a water spectacle that likely won't happen again for a long time. Not to mention, I want him to try my new drink."

"It's dangerous, Max. Vick is just waiting for him to show his face."

"We'll sneak him in the back, Vick won't see. After the competition, you and he can leave early. Come on. He'll love it."

I knew Max was right. "Let me talk to Ciro, and I'll keep in touch."

He went to his car and I to mine. It was nice driving home, knowing someone was there. And as I turned onto my street, I called Ciro to ask him his thoughts on it.

"We can make sure he's safe. Get a guy to stay at his section." And just like that, I had some good news to tell Toby.

———

"Do I look dumb?" Toby was wearing a dress shirt that matched the color of his sling and a silver jacket with dark pants.

"You look amazing, now stop." Chuckling, I went back to getting my braids into a ponytail. It worked with my outfit and gave me a slicker appearance.

"You look amazing in purple." Toby slid a finger along the width of my shoulders, making me shiver.

"It's my favorite color too, how lucky for me."

"I'm so excited to go out. Thanks for asking me, and I promise I won't leave my section. I can't wait to see this live." He was practically vibrating with excitement, and it was contagious.

"I knew we'd find use for the water."

Toby's smile dropped for a second. "You're sure everything is going to be okay with the event and everything?"

"Yeah, why?"

"When I told Vick about you coming up with a cool show and all the things I could tell him about Joker's Sin, he got excited. If he found out about tonight, he might've done something."

Yeah, I remembered Toby telling me he had to tell Vick certain things and thought of the most useless of information. "I think he planned on doing something the night of that bachelor party, but I never let his guys in, so it was ruined. But we're taking every precaution. I promise."

Toby had a thoughtful expression, then shrugged. "I suppose that makes some logical sense. I feel like I'm paranoid."

We parked on the side of the club; it was early, so no one was there yet besides Max, Ledger, and Ciro.

"I feel like I've been gone forever," Toby said as we stepped into the club.

"Well, let me know if it seems different," I joked, glad when he smiled.

Toby was greeted by the guys all asking how he was. He had painkillers but said he didn't want to take them because he didn't want to pass out and miss anything, so he was using extra-strength aspirin for the evening. I told him to let me know by texting me if he needed to go home and if it got to be too much. He just huffed, which I took as agreement.

Before the doors opened, Toby walked around, talked to staff, and laughed…a lot. With everything going on, it was good to see a smile on his face more often than not.

Ledger announced doors were opening, and Toby slowly made his way upstairs, two of Ciro's security guys in tow. If Toby had to go to the bathroom, anything at all, he always had eyes on him. Of course when I told Toby that, he said he didn't want anyone to stare at him while he pissed.

I knew he'd be okay up there, but I kept my cell phone tucked tightly in my pants pocket. There were tablets on the bar where people would be able to enter their names in to be in the running as a dancer for the competition. Ledger would put it through a random app, and ten would be chosen.

I made my way to the stage to begin the night's festivities.

"Hello, hello, hello, one and all, and welcome to Wet and Wild Wednesday!" Cheers erupted, I looked up and saw Toby's bright smile, and I was truly glad he was there tonight.

I explained the rules of the competition, what the winner got, and how they entered. "In an hour the ten people will be announced, and you'll make your way to the back to get dressed."

It was a mad scramble of people trying to get their names in, and Ledger cranked the music. I stepped down until it was time to reveal those chosen.

I went up to the VIP area, Max's drink of the night in hand, greeted people up there, talked, loved hearing how they were excited to see the show, then made my way over to Toby, who was talking to one of the security guys.

"Everyone is so freaking thrilled!" He was doing this little hop thing, like he couldn't contain his enthusiasm. I handed him the drink, which he sipped, releasing a hum of approval.

"It's going to be a hell of a show."

I was able to sit and have a drink with him before Ledger texted me that it was time to call out the names. Toby wished me good luck and gave me a peck on my cheek that made me want to close the curtain and ask for more. But, reluctantly, I made my way down the stairs and onto the stage to announce the names.

What I loved about the ten chosen was the diversity of them. Not all were skinny or had a good body. They were in all shapes and sizes, and I knew they'd each find a jumpsuit that fit their body. When they went to the back, I spoke with the crowd some more, asked what song Ledger should play, even though he had the one he was doing set to go.

By the time the ten dancers returned, the room was buzzing, the people anxious to see the amazing show. The clear walls came up, and before I stepped off the stage, I held my arms out wide and shouted, "Let it rain!"

CHAPTER THIRTY-TWO

Toby

If I had mobility in both arms, I would've been clapping when Atlas shouted, "Let it rain!" Everyone cheered, and damn, the place came alive whenever he was in the spotlight.

The second he stepped off the stage, Ledger began the music. He was behind a waterproof booth built for the night, and the ten dancers were all spread along the area, ready for some serious fun. They were smiling and laughing and the second the beat got to them, they were unstoppable dancing machines.

One of the guys who was in the VIP section with me said he had to run downstairs; there was an issue in one of the bathrooms, and Ciro couldn't locate some guy named Dean. I waved him away, drank the delicious beverage Max made, and watched the show.

Atlas was walking up to the VIP area when the rain started. Slowly. This was only going to be lasting one song, so I knew it would pick up, and those suits would get see-through fast.

"Are they wearing boxers or anything under there?" I asked Atlas as he came up beside me.

"Speedos." He laughed. "Each with a flirty word printed on their butts, so when they get wet people see it."

I tore my eyes away from the stage to give Atlas my attention. He was radiant, glowing, he loved what he did, and he was made to be doing it.

"Atlas, I—"

I wasn't sure exactly what I was going to say, but it didn't matter because the sound of painful screams coming from the stage grabbed my attention. Turning, I saw the dancers were all covering their faces, one was on the ground, and the music had stopped.

"Shut off the water!" I heard Ledger shout into the mic.

"Doesn't he have the button?" I asked and realized it clearly wasn't working.

Atlas rushed down the stairs, likely going to the manual lever, and the security guy and I followed after him.

The shouts and screams became louder, and it sounded like a stampede of people were racing somewhere.

"Help me," Atlas shouted as he tried to pull the lever. Three guys helped, and soon the water was shut off.

Not a second later, Atlas was racing out of the room and to the stage. "What the fuck, Ledger?"

"It was fine, they were dancing. Then they just started screaming and…" He gestured to the people on the stage, moaning, crying, and screaming.

One of them lifted their head and I could see their face. Bright red rings around their eyes and splotchy skin made it appear like burns.

"Atlas," I shouted.

"What?"

"Call an ambulance, we need to wash their eyes out, we need clean water. Look."

When he saw them, he turned gray. "It's like they were maced or something."

"Exactly, come on."

"I'll call," Ledger said.

"Get Max to help me. You need to calm everyone, Atlas."

He nodded. "Take the security guys too, you can all help one person each. There's a shower in my office too, use it if you need to."

It was awkward with one arm, but I was able to get one of the guys to the bathroom. Max handed us cups as we passed, and when I was in the bathroom, I instructed him to lift his head up.

"I'm going to wash your eyes, and it won't be fun, sorry."

Halfway through, EMTs arrived and took over. When the police and fire department got there, the whole place was shut down. I was soaking wet from the waist to my feet when I walked out of the bathroom and saw Atlas speaking with a firefighter and police officer.

"How are they?" Atlas asked when I approached.

"It's too soon. The EMTs are with them." I said hello to the fireman and police officer.

"What happened to you?" the cop asked, no doubt my arm in a sling and the bruising on my face raised that question.

"What happened to me was an issue with a past employer, Vick Keller." I didn't know why I was feeling brave all of a sudden, but I knew in my gut this was all his doing. "The same person you may want to look into about what happened here today."

"That's a serious allegation, Mr—"

"Toby St. Claire."

When the cop's eyes widened, I knew he was aware of things, and that likely meant he was working with Vick. The fireman didn't react at all.

"Thank you, Mr. St. Claire, we will take that under advisement. Do you need medical attention?"

I told the fireman no and went to sit at the bar while Atlas finished up. It was going to be a long night.

———

WE DIDN'T GET BACK to Atlas's place until six in the morning. We were exhausted, and Atlas was beyond pissed. They informed him they had to shut his club down for at least a week to investigate. No Joker's Sin for a week. I bet Vick was loving that.

"I didn't mean to throw Vick's name out there like that," I said as I plopped on the couch. My clothes had long since dried, thank goodness.

"That's the least of our problems." He sat beside me, and my heart did a little flip when he rested his hand on my knee. Stupid I was sure, but that simple touch was needed.

"We need to clean up and pass out," he said as he rested his head against the cushion.

"Or we can just pass out and wash later."

He rolled his head, facing me. "Wanna take a nap with me on the couch?"

I wanted it more than anything at that moment. "Yeah."

He lifted a small console on the other side of him and pushed the button, reclining the couch and extending its footrests.

"Fancy."

He laughed, and within seconds his eyes were closed. I rested my head on his shoulder, my arm secure, but couldn't find sleep as easily.

My mind was racing with everything that happened tonight, and the more I thought about it, the more I could see Vick was behind it all. On the ride over to Atlas's place, I told him how all the dots connected. From an unexplained water delivery, to Vick being glad to hear about everything I told him about Joker's Sin, and the other night when Atlas said a few of Vick's men got into the club. Sure, he said he got them out before anything happened, but maybe one was able to fuck with the mechanics, and that was why Ledger couldn't shut the water off. There were too many variables, and they all pointed at one person: Vick Keller. Maybe I wasn't as paranoid as I thought.

With Atlas fast asleep, I focused on his breathing and within minutes, I was closing my eyes. Surprisingly, we slept for a solid six hours before our phones started going off.

For me it was Poppy, asking what was going on and me having to explain everything I knew. Of course she agreed about Vick being responsible. For Atlas it was Max and Ledger, a police officer, and his lawyer. We spent the rest of our day dealing with everyone and by that evening, we were spent and ready for the day to just end. There was nothing more we could do at that point, and we were good and done.

Regardless of anything, tomorrow was coming…whether we were ready for it or not.

CHAPTER THIRTY-THREE

Atlas

Ciro arrived at my apartment that afternoon, said he heard from TJ, and she would certainly have news by the end of the week. Knowing I'd have to wait made me realize how much of my life was consumed by Joker's Sin. Without handling club business Toby and I hung around the apartment. It was nice having him there, I just wished it wasn't out of fear.

When Friday came, I had to take Toby to the doctor, where we were hoping the sling could come off. Part of me was glad he would have the use of both his arms; the other part was fear. I kept putting off doing more with Toby because of his arm and not wanting to hurt him—at least that was what I told him. Every passing day my feelings for him grew. I loved how he ate, laughed, told jokes and messed them up. Even seeing him sleep-rumpled in the morning or cursing out his sling was adorable. And amid the seriousness of what happened at Joker's Sin, I was able to find happiness with Toby. And the only other person who'd ever had that power was Joker.

Just thinking his name made my heart ache, and an odd

twinge of betrayal twisted my gut. I knew it was ridiculous to think I was cheating on him, but I couldn't help it.

"Good news. I think you can take this off, but you're going to need to start PT," the orthopedic doctor said.

"Oh, thank heavens." Toby smiled so brightly.

"If you give me a list of therapists, I'll make an appointment."

"Sure, head over to reception, and I'll have it printed out."

I told Toby I'd meet him there, and I went and got the list. A few stated they traveled, and I knew I'd feel better if they came to my place instead of taking Toby to them. Especially with us all having bullseyes on our head.

"All set?" Toby asked as he joined me.

"Yep, how's it feel?"

Shrugging, he said, "Little sore but wow, I'm so glad to be free of it." He held the sling in his hand. "He said if it starts to be too sore or after PT, I may need it."

Fair enough. "How about we grab something for lunch and eat it at my place?"

We stepped outside, and the gorgeous sun shone down on us. "It's beautiful out, can't we just eat it in the park?" He pointed to the park across from the hospital.

I hated being out in the open, but then again, it was broad daylight, and the park was filled with people. There were food carts all around, so I agreed it would be nice. We made our way over, each getting a hot dog and fries with a water, and sat under a tree.

It was easy to tell Toby was happy to be free of the sling. He hummed with each bite and lifted his face to the sun. I almost forgot to eat, I was so lost in how stunning and carefree he was in that moment.

When Toby caught me gawking, he simply smiled. I didn't look away, and in that quiet moment, with the sun streaming on us, I knew I wasn't going to be able to escape my feelings for him.

———

"So, no sling." Toby tossed the offending contraption onto my couch and quirked his lips. "I was thinking."

"Well, that's dangerous." Thirsty, I went to my kitchen to get a glass of water, and Toby followed.

"Atlas, I know we can't go anywhere, really. I mean we can, but self-preservation and all that."

I chuckled and retrieved a glass, filling it. "Right, go on."

"I guess what I'm asking…" He took a couple of steps toward me until he was only a few inches from my body, and I could feel his electricity, how it wrapped around me. "Atlas, I'd like to cook for you tonight, and I want to call it a date."

It was a good thing I'd swallowed the water, or I would've choked. He was so sincere, and that familiar terror of betrayal beat against my chest. But, there was really no reason to tell him no.

"Okay, sure. That sounds nice, Toby."

He did this little excited hop, clapped his hands together, and winced. "Okay, no clapping yet, but yay!"

I chuckled, drained my water, and grinned. "Need help?"

"Nope. I got this, it's all me, shoo, skedaddle!"

"Well, it's only two in the afternoon, you need to start now?"

He looked at the clock and bit his lip. "Okay, so maybe not skedaddle yet."

I did end up spending an hour in the kitchen with Toby while he asked me a million questions about allergies, likes and dislikes, and by the end of it, I had no idea what he was planning on making.

"Okay, go get ready. I'm going to cook and then inform you when our date is to begin."

With a shake of my head and a grin, I did as I was told. I showered slowly, then chose something comfortable but nice for our date. Every few minutes that familiar pang of guilt and sadness would hit, but I'd push it down. I didn't know if Joker would like Toby. I did know that I did and while there was baggage with Toby, and he'd lied, it wasn't anything like what Joker did. But I loved Joker still, and breaking away from that was hard.

When I was ready, I went and sat in the living room, turned on the news, and waited. The aroma was mouthwatering, and I knew it was going to be delicious. I couldn't remember the last time anyone had cooked for me outside of going to a restaurant.

I had assumed Toby was in the kitchen, but when he stepped out of the guest room, wearing a wine-colored long-sleeved shirt and khakis, with his hair styled and just a hint of make-up, he surprised me.

"Oh," he said. "You look amazing."

I stood and moved closer to him, loving how he craned his neck to meet my eyes. "You're looking pretty damn amazing yourself." I met his lips in a chaste kiss, not wanting to get too lost in him quite yet. I needed to go slow for me, and knowing Toby was still healing, I didn't want to hurt him.

"I hope you're hungry." His tone was flirty, indicating he didn't just mean for food.

"Famished."

"Good, let's eat and see where the night takes us."

He'd made a delicious lemon-pepper chicken with wild rice and carrots. There were biscuits, and he must've found a bottle of wine, because it rested in a bucket of ice. I had a small table in the kitchen which he had set for two and for a brief moment, it was hard to breathe. It was more than just a dinner tonight. I knew that.

"Looks and smells incredible."

He beamed. "Sit, I'll get everything."

As much as I wanted to help him, I knew he was loving doing all this; the sheer look of joy on his face told me that. So, I sat as he plated our food, and when he was sitting across from me, I took a breath.

"Wine?" I asked.

"Oh, yes!"

I filled our glasses, and we began eating. We talked about why he chose purple highlights in his hair, and then I explained to him the process of washing my braids. He found that insanely interesting and asked a million questions. It was light and we laughed a lot. I could've stayed in that moment forever.

CHAPTER THIRTY-FOUR

Toby

Being stuck inside for our own safety had never been so amazing. For a short time, I was able to forget all the threats beyond the penthouse. I had Atlas's undivided attention, and while I wouldn't have wanted anything to ever happen to Joker's Sin, I was grateful to have his company.

"That was delicious, Toby." Atlas wiped his mouth and relaxed in his chair.

"Thanks." I wanted to get up, walk over to him, and straddle his lap. But I also wanted to have him on his back and lick every inch of him.

"What do we do next on this date?"

I had options here. I could play coy, ask him to watch a movie, cuddle, hoping it went to dirty fabulous places. Or I could just go for broke.

"I want to have you for dessert," I blurted out. Me forgetting how to use words was becoming some sort of thing when I was around Atlas and sex was involved.

He blinked, but nothing else. "Is that right?" Scanning my face, he smirked. "And where would you have me?"

Oh, shit. For real? He's going to let me have him? "Not here."

Atlas took pity on me, stood, and held out his hand. "Come with me."

I slid my hand in his and followed him, not knowing where he was going to take me at first, but when he started leading me down the hallway to where his bedroom was, happy horny butter-flies began dancing in my stomach.

I had given Atlas his privacy the entire time I was here; the few times we messed around were in the bathroom, my room, or the living room. When he was at work, I never went into his bedroom and snooped. That wasn't who I was. So when I stepped foot into his room for the first time, it was everything I thought it would be. Splashes of purple and black painted the walls, a deep plum-colored comforter adorned the bed. Large windows, like the rest of the place, were framed by black curtains. The city twinkled and the moon was full.

"Where do you want me?" he asked.

"Um…bed, yeah, bed, totally bed."

He chuckled and sat, clothes and all.

Oh, my God. I've had sex before. Why am I so nervous?

"Now what?"

"Shit, I'm messing this up."

He crooked his finger in a "come here" gesture. "Let me help you."

I wanted that. I stepped between his spread legs. His hands slid behind my thighs, cupping my ass.

"How about we get rid of our clothes and go from there?" I nodded, because yeah, words weren't my friends.

With the same slow pace, we removed our clothes. I could tell Atlas wanted to help me, especially when it came to getting my sore arm out of the sleeve, but he watched and let me do it. With each article he removed, I marveled at his beauty. Atlas Durand was stunning.

His dark skin glowed as the moonlight shone over his bare chest. He lifted his butt and slid his pants and boxers off in one go, and there he was, naked. He pushed back against his comforter, arms folded behind his head, and he arched a brow.

"You gonna finish getting all naked for me, Toby?"

"I…" *Words, right.* I quickly divested myself of the rest of my clothes and took one step, then two. Shit, even his feet were pretty.

"You okay?"

"You're…shit, Atlas, I'm not sure there are words to describe what's going through my head right now." Gliding my hand along his ankle, letting his hair tickle my palm, made it so much more real. He was here, naked on his bed. For me.

"Maybe show me, then."

He spread his legs wider so I could climb between them. I didn't need any more invitation than that. I made sure to take my time and not put too much weight on my bad arm. He grinned, but the lust and fire in his eyes gave me courage.

"You're beautiful, Toby."

I rolled my eyes and huffed. "I've got more colors on my skin than a rainbow."

He sat up suddenly, cupped my face in his hands, and pressed his lips to mine. I fell into him, his taste, his tongue, his breath.

He pulled away, and his honey-brown eyes were intense. "Even if you were orange with pink polka dots, I'd think you were beautiful. Don't doubt that." He took my hand and placed it on his erection. "You do this to me, Toby."

Gripping his cock, I moved my hand along his hard, velvety flesh. His eyelids fluttered, and when he moaned, I felt powerful. He wanted me.

"Lie back." He did as I asked, craning his neck up against the pillows as I moved faster over his shaft. Precome glistened at the tip, and I wanted to taste him. Leaning in, I flicked my tongue over the head, bittersweetness bursting on my tongue, and I wanted so much more.

I moved my hand to cup his balls and suck his cock as deeply as I could. Atlas fisted his bedspread and it fed me, drove me, made me want him to come down my throat.

"Shit," he moaned.

His balls tightened, and I could tell he was seconds away from coming. I picked up the pace; I loved his taste, how he felt, and I wanted his come as much as he wanted to give it to me.

He arched up slightly, and then that bittersweetness exploded in my mouth, and I swallowed as fast as I could. When I'd sucked every drop, I licked up his shaft until he hissed.

"Sensitive."

"Best dessert ever," I said, and he laughed.

"Hmm…I'm still hungry."

Fuck, and so was I. "What are you hungry for?"

He lifted up, leaning on his elbow. "More, Toby. I think I'm always going to want more with you."

There was a deep sadness in Atlas's eyes; I knew it was his own memories, his own ghosts. I was a lot of things—an idiot wasn't one of them. He was feeling a lot toward me, and it terrified him. If I were a betting man, I'd bet he only slept with people to scratch an itch, but Joker was the last person he'd fucked that he cared about.

"I want you inside me, Atlas."

His smile was so small. And before he said anything he might regret, I spoke. "But I'm not him. I'm not Joker. I'm not that guy Lance either, or anyone who scratched an itch for you. I don't want you to fuck me, Atlas, I want you to make love to me, Toby St. Claire. I want you to wake up in the morning and not regret it. I want you to be able to let the ghosts go. Can you do that?"

He took a breath, his gaze moving to the window, toward the city that took more from him than it had given.

"When I close my eyes, I see him. I don't want to, but I don't know how to not see him, hear him, feel him."

I moved closer and straddled his waist. He met my gaze; so much pain took residence there.

"Don't close your eyes, Atlas. Look at me, see me, feel me, hear me."

"I want that."

"Be with me, okay?"

He nodded, and a single tear slipped out and slid along his cheek. I wiped it away with my thumb, leaned down, and took him in a kiss that I hoped expressed how much I understood, how I wasn't going anywhere. When I sat up, his eyes were on me.

"I won't close them," he whispered.

CHAPTER THIRTY-FIVE

Atlas

With my arms wrapped around Toby, I spun us so I hovered over him. Making sure I watched his features for any winces of pain, I received only a yelp of surprise.

I kept replaying Toby's words, the truth and understanding painted on his face. This wasn't just sex for me; it was mixing emotions with a physical act I'd done more times than I cared to admit. When we were both sated, I wouldn't get up and leave or ask him to leave. This was going to mean something—not just to me but to him.

Leaning into Toby, I took his lips in a punishing kiss. The man consumed me, and with our chests together, the pounding of his heart echoed my own. He hooked one arm around my neck, and the other slid over my ass cheek.

"You feel amazing," Toby said as I nestled into his neck, tasting his skin.

"So do you."

When he wrapped his legs around my waist and rutted against my hardening cock, I bit just enough to make him gasp. Our mixed precome made our dicks slick, and the slide was gonna make me come if I didn't stop.

"Please, Atlas."

I knew what he wanted, and I wanted it too. I reached over to my nightstand and grabbed lube and a condom, tossing them onto the bed. Working my way down his body, I stopped when I reached the crease of his groin. He watched me, and I made sure to look him in the eyes at every moment. Lifting a leg, I was glad when he spread the other, leaving himself completely exposed for me.

"Hand me the lube?" I asked, and when he reached for it, I slid my tongue along his groin, over his shaft until I was lapping at his balls.

"Shit, Atlas…" He chuckled, struggling to grip the lube.

He finally handed it to me, but I was taking my time with Toby. I sucked, licked, and devoured him until he was vibrating. There was a fine sheen of sweat covering his skin, and he was writhing beautifully.

I sat up, poured lube on my fingers and over his hole, gently rubbing it. The whole time, Toby watched me. Biting his lip and moaning as I pushed my fingers inside him, pumping and readying him for my cock. Pleas fell from his lips, and when I couldn't wait any longer, I sheathed my cock and so, so slowly pushed into his heat.

"Oh fuck," he whispered against my lips. I kissed his moans, his prayers for more.

He met me each time I slammed into him, and when I reached between our bodies, taking his cock in my hand, his orgasm hit, and he spilled over my fingers. I chased my own, only seconds behind him. Bracing my arms on either side of him, I arched up, pushing into him as far as I could, and shouted as I came.

After I pulled out, slipped the condom off, and tossed it, I told Toby to stay there and I'd get him cleaned up. He mumbled through a serene expression. I went to the bathroom, got a warm washcloth, and when I returned to the bed I chuckled. He hadn't moved an inch, and he was smiling at me.

"Your smile does things to me." I gently washed away his drying come.

"Good things, I hope."

"Very, very good things."

After tossing the washcloth into the laundry bin and placing the lube in the nightstand, I pulled the comforter back, scooped Toby up in my arms, and tucked us both under it.

"That was the best date ever," Toby slurred, exhaustion taking over.

"Agreed."

———

I woke to my cell phone going off. Toby was snug in my arms, so I reached behind me and snagged it. Ciro.

"Hey."

"Hey, so TJ got a good hit on something. Can we come by your place this afternoon?" Pulling the phone away from my ear, I saw the clock read nine thirty.

"Yeah, how about noon? We can have lunch here."

"Sounds like a plan. See ya later."

"Everything okay?" Toby's voice was muffled with sleep.

"Yeah. Ciro and that detective, TJ, are coming at noon. He says she has something to tell us."

He nodded but a second later, his soft snores were filling the room. As carefully as possible, I slid my arm out from under him. My bladder was protesting, and as much as I wanted to stay ensconced in bed with him, nature called.

I ended up showering, changing, and making coffee. I was on my second cup when a sleep-rumpled Toby entered the kitchen.

"Mmm coffee." He shuffled over to the coffeepot and fixed a mug.

"Sleep well?" I asked when he joined me at the table. I'd had to clean it this morning, seeing as we didn't bother to after dinner, but it was well worth it.

"Best sleep in a long time." He sipped his coffee with a grin.

"Same."

We sat in companionable silence, drinking coffee and eating some toast I made. Being the late morning hour, neither of us wanted to be full for lunch.

Toby left to shower and change while I called Vayne's, our favorite restaurant, to place an order to be delivered for twelve.

Toby had just stepped out of his room when there was a knock on the door. Although Ciro had clearance to come up, no one but me had a key to my apartment. When I opened the door, Ciro and TJ stood there and the delivery guy too.

"You ordered from Vayne's?" Ciro asked.

"Yeah, didn't feel like cooking for you." I let TJ and Ciro in and took the bag from the delivery guy. I'd already paid and tipped when I ordered.

I opted for my living room, where we could all sit comfortably. Toby got drinks while the rest of us set up the lunches.

As we ate, I filled TJ in on what happened at the club on Wednesday. Most she was aware of. I told her I wouldn't be permitted to reopen until the investigation was complete, and I was cleared of any wrongdoing. She said she'd keep an ear to the ground and see if she could find anything out.

Once we were all done eating, I cleaned up and brought coffee out.

"Hopefully you have some good news for us," I said, handing her a mug.

"Thanks. I think I do."

When I started out in Haven Hart and made shitty business

decisions, I vowed never to get into bed with criminals or unscrupulous people again. I knew with every passing year how impossible that promise was to keep. I wanted to save my club and keep Toby and his sister safe, and to do that, I was going to have to get my hands dirty.

"Let's hear it."

CHAPTER THIRTY-SIX

Toby

TJ took out a tablet and began explaining her plan. "Like I said earlier, we need Vick to go head-to-head with someone bigger and more powerful than himself. He needs to piss someone off who wouldn't blink at making him disappear."

"Wait," I interrupted. "You're actually one of the good guys?"

She chuckled as did Ciro. "I learned a long time ago, there's a way to take out the trash in this town, and the straight and narrow isn't it. But I'd never take money or meddle in drugs. What Vick Keller is doing to you, your sister, and Atlas, won't come to an end the old-fashioned way. He has too many cops on his payroll. So, we need to fight fire with fire."

"Doesn't fighting fire with fire just make more fire?" I asked, and she gave me an indulgent smile.

"You're gonna have to trust me just a little here." I shut up, sat back, and heard her out.

"Vick Keller has partial control on the docks over here." She put the tablet down, showing a section of the inlet where a lot of shipments came in. I knew that well from the story Shane told me about Chester being beaten and strung up on the shipping crate.

"However, Wang Zhao pays Vick Keller a good amount to let his ships unload over there. The manifest always reads organic chemicals, but it's drugs."

"Wang Zhao is the boss of the Chinese gang. Don't they own all the way from Graham Boulevard to Richmond Avenue?" Atlas asked.

"Yes, he has a huge chunk of space. And he's smart with the other bosses. They keep the peace and because of that, we don't have full-on gunfights in the streets."

"But if Vick works for Wang, how's this gonna work?" I asked.

"How Wang has it set up, shipment comes in and Vick has it unloaded, separated, and sent over to Wang. Now, this is where it gets tricky. We can't just sit on the docks and bombard them. Vick has like, fifteen guys unloading. But"—she held up a finger—"once it's all in the truck, it's just two guys until it gets over to Wang's; then his guys take it."

"Okay, so that's even more guys." I hoped I wasn't sounding dumb.

"What you're saying is, between the docks and Wang's, we fuck up the stuff," Ciro said.

"It's coke," TJ said. "If we have something almost comparable to the naked eye and hijack the truck and replace it, when Wang checks it out, he'll think Vick is stealing from him for his own financial gain."

"Ummm…yeah, how do we do any of this? First off, I've never even let my license expire, let alone done a heist. Also, what do we do with Vick's guys?" I hated being a downer on this, but it had to be said.

"I agree with Toby here, how do we get this to work?" Atlas reached over and squeezed my hand. His support meant a lot.

"Vick's guys will have to disappear. Leave that part to me. When faced with jail time, most of these guys fold. Vick doesn't pay them enough for their loyalty. When Vick's guys don't return, he'll try to blame them for it, but Wang won't care. Vick will have to pay the price."

Made sense but… "And who is doing this? We can't have the cops involved."

"Not all the cops are on Vick's payroll, and TJ here has a few she trusts. They'll fill in as Vick's guys." Ciro was very matter-of-fact.

"When is all this taking place?" Atlas asked. I could see how worried he was about everything.

"Wang has a delivery Sunday. So that night, Vick's guys will go over to the docks and unload. That's when we do this." TJ picked up her tablet. "If Vick is too busy trying not to start a war with Wang, it gets him off your back. But the thing about Wang is, he's ruthless. Even if Vick comes up with the money or the coke, he won't spare him. If he can kill his own son, he won't blink at taking out Vick."

"He killed his own kid?" I asked, heartbroken.

"Yeah. He's a piece of shit, like most of the scum in this city."

"You don't think this will backfire on Atlas or me or anyone?" I had to wonder. While Vick would try to put out fires, the coincidence this was all happening after he tried to destroy Atlas's business wouldn't go unnoticed.

"We're going to have to hope Wang deals with him before he realizes any of that. It's not a perfect plan, but it's the best one we have right now." TJ gave us a sympathetic smile, but I knew she was right, and judging by Ciro's and Atlas's faces, they did too.

"Okay."

TJ and Ciro left shortly after that and told us they'd be in touch. My shoulder was sore, so Atlas said he'd run a warm bath, we could soak a bit, and then rest in bed and watch a movie. That sounded like the best idea in a long time.

———

"It's weird not seeing you every day," I said to Poppy late Saturday afternoon. She and Desi came over shortly after Ciro and TJ left, because we missed each other. Atlas and Desi were watching a baseball game on TV, and Poppy and I were drinking coffee and catching up in the kitchen.

"I know. But, it's not so bad." Her cheeks pinked, a dead give-away something was up.

"Care to tell me more, sister mine?"

She chuckled. "I really like Desi, and Toby, I think he likes me a lot too. He's, like, the first guy in forever that sees me and not the chair."

I'd had a feeling something was going on with them. "That's wonderful."

"Yeah? I was worried to say anything to you. But, he's sweet. The other day, we went out to dinner to this little Italian place. It was on the bottom floor, and there were no elevators." There'd been so many times Poppy and I had to go elsewhere due to lack of proper handicap accessibility.

"I'm sorry, Poppy."

"No, no, no, shut up and listen." I chuckled, and she powered through her story. "Without missing a beat, he scooped me up, walked me down the stairs, and asked the hostess for a table for two. Now it's hard for me to sit in those shitty wooden chairs, so when she took us to our table, he said they had to go get my chair at the top of the stairs." She was laughing so hard at this point, it was hard to follow her story.

"The hostess was all, 'We don't do that,' so Desi said, 'Well, it's illegal not to have handicap accessibility,' and told her if they didn't want to be reported she'd get my fucking chair there, pronto."

I loved seeing her so happy, and it sounded like Desi was amazing to her. "He sounds like a keeper."

She smiled and nodded. "Yeah." She eyed where Desi and Atlas were sitting. "What about you and The Greatest Showman?"

"Ha ha, you're funny. We're good…great, even."

Her brows shot up to her hairline. "Yeah?"

"Yeah, but it's early days. He's working through some stuff and the shit with the club. We're taking it a day at a time."

She took my hand in hers. "That's the best way to do it."

Desi and Poppy left shortly after dinner, and after I shut the front door, I walked over to where Atlas was sitting on the couch, kneeled between his legs, and began to unbuckle his pants.

"Whatcha doing on the floor?" He grinned.

"You, I hope."

"Far be it from me to stand in the way of someone so determined."

I chuckled and slid his pants down to his ankles. His cock was hard, and my mouth watered.

"Oh, and I'm very fucking determined." Nothing more was said as I took him into my mouth, sucked him to the root, and didn't let up until I was swallowing every drop.

CHAPTER THIRTY-SEVEN

Atlas

Having Poppy and Desi come over on Saturday helped pass some time, but Toby and I were going a little stir-crazy. Whenever we spoke with Ciro, he told us we couldn't do anything but be unseen. His explanation made sense, of course. If Toby or I, or even any of my guys, were seen near this, Vick would absolutely link us to it.

When Sunday morning came, we were feeling a little caged in, so Toby and I went down to the farmers market. I didn't like being so exposed, but the truth of it was, we needed to get out. Don't get me wrong, the copious amounts of sex we had to pass time was amazing, but we needed air and sunshine.

"Oh, look at this." Toby held up a sculpture made from blown glass…a very phallic sculpture.

I slid my finger over the smooth object. "Are you trying to tell me you're not satisfied?"

He bit his bottom lip, and without a thought, I kissed him. In front of everyone around I did it. Whereas normally I'd think it through, not want to lead anyone on or have anyone know someone meant anything to me. With Toby, everything washed away, and I only cared about what not showing him how I felt would do to him.

"I'm not sure the families in the area want to watch such a depraved act out in the open. What do you think, Liberio?" Vick Keller's voice was like ice water on our lukewarm moment.

I spun around, instinctively pushing Toby behind me.

"Disgusting." Liberio sneered.

"Trust me that these families would rather see a drug peddling, degenerate like you disappear long before me."

Vick started laughing obnoxiously, parents with their kids moving out of the way fairly quickly. "How's business?" he asked when he calmed.

"Opens back up soon. You know," I said, crossing my arms over my chest, "I should thank you. Joker's Sin has so much more attention now, which I didn't think was possible, seeing how popular it already was. And, the insurance company is paying for some damages, so I can renovate a little. Make it even more amazing." I stared him down, finding joy when a twitch formed in his cheek.

"I told you I wasn't playing games, Atlas."

"And yet here you are, in the middle of the market…playing."

If there weren't so many people around, I was sure either Vick or Liberio would've tried to punch me. But they both curled their lips, grunted something, and stormed away.

"Do you really think egging him on like that was smart?" Toby slid his hand in mine.

"What's he gonna do, Toby? Try to destroy my business, hurt you? Oh look, he's done that." I leaned closer to his ear and whispered, "After tonight, I'm hoping Vick Keller isn't a problem for us anymore."

"For both our sakes, I hope you're right."

Later in the afternoon, Ciro came by my place to go over

everything happening that night. TJ was with her guys preparing, so it was just the three of us here.

"What are they using instead of the coke?" Toby asked as he set three mugs of coffee down.

Ciro's grin told me he was about to give us a lesson. He surprised me sometimes with what he knew and what he'd done in his life.

"I'm not sure how much you know about cocaine, but Hollywood hasn't exactly been honest with its portrayal."

Toby sipped his coffee. "So, like, it's not white or…?"

"It can be when it's mixed with like, talcum powder or something like that. But it's generally a beige or almost pinkish color. Wang's does happen to be white, but we suspect it's something that they do before they ship it here. Thank God too—we wouldn't have time for a coloring process."

"So they're gonna look at it, shrug, and it's over?" Toby asked.

"No. Wang isn't a fucking idiot. He will have it tested, and that's how it becomes tricky. We have to fool them long enough that they'll let our guys go. He does this quick test, and because he's worked with Vick so long, his guys won't suspect foul play right away."

Ciro sat back with his mug, but Toby wasn't done. I had to smile at how inquisitive he was.

"So if you use flour or whatever, and they taste it, won't they know? I mean I've never done drugs in my life, but I'm sure it has a unique taste."

Ciro nodded. "It does. It tends to actually have a smell too. Sometimes it's a sweet smell with a chemical twinge to it. I did get my hands on Wang's product, and it has a sweeter smell to it, not super pungent in the chemical department. Reminded me of a perfume my mother wore once, so I grabbed that. Sprayed my hands with it and ran them through the powder. Not overpowering but passable."

"And the taste?"

"So many questions." Ciro chuckled. "Okay, the taste is kinda what it smells like. When you test cocaine, you generally rub it over your gums. It's the quickest way to test for purity. Uncut cocaine will numb the gums. Obviously ours isn't even near to being cocaine, so we mixed the powder with a numbing agent. It'll be convincing enough to get TJ's guys out of there."

"Wow," Toby whispered. "You're terrifying, Ciro."

"Only 'cause I have to be."

Ciro ended up staying. He was in contact with TJ, and I think he wasn't one hundred percent convinced one of us wouldn't leave the penthouse to head to the docks.

For the most part, the evening was quiet. We watched a movie, ordered pizza. It was boring but safe. We weren't near the shit, and even though I wanted to end Vick myself, knowing that if our plan worked Wang would make him go away appeased me enough to let myself be bored.

It was close to midnight when Ciro's phone buzzed. He read whatever it was and texted something back. It went that way for a while. Toby and I looked at each other and shrugged.

"So?" I asked when he stood and slipped his phone into his pocket.

"Went off without a hitch. TJ has Vick's guys, and they'll be on the first plane out of here."

"Now what do we do?" Toby sat up, peering at Ciro imploringly.

"Now we wait. Wang will realize what's happened, and that's when the fireworks begin." He pointed to the two of us. "Go about your lives like you don't know. I'm sure Joker's Sin will be cleared. TJ said the investigation concluded. You probably want to focus on that."

I nodded and got off the couch. "Yeah. Thanks, Ciro. Be safe out there."

"Always am. Night, Toby."

"Night."

Even though I knew Toby was as exhausted as I felt, sleep wasn't going to come easy to me.

"Want to go to bed?" I asked Toby as I offered him my hand.

"I don't think I could sleep."

I pulled him off the couch, pressing his smaller body to mine.

"Who said we needed to sleep?"

His smile was all the consent I needed. I scooped him up, his legs wrapping around my waist, and carried him to my bedroom.

CHAPTER THIRTY-EIGHT

Toby

Atlas and I tumbled to the bed, our mouths fused together, only parting to remove our clothes. My insides felt like a growing knot of anxiety, worry, fear, and sadness over everything going on. But when Atlas licked his way into my mouth, when his hands glided along my skin, it was like he was wiping away every negative emotion.

The room quickly filled with moans, grunts, and heavy breathing. I loved how we smelled together, felt together, were together.

"How's your shoulder?" Atlas asked as he slid his tongue over my nipple, heading toward my stomach.

"Fine, fuck."

He chuckled and then took my cock in his mouth with quick, hollowed thrusts, and I could feel my orgasm rising to the surface.

"Atlas."

My cock fell from his lips, and he practically folded me in half. "What the…?" I didn't get another word out. His mouth sealed over my hole in the dirtiest kiss I'd ever had. His tongue kept plunging inside, and I swear I could've died right then and there and been fine with it.

"You taste so sweet," he said, eyes on fire, lips glistening with spit.

"Fuck, Atlas, please, please fuck me."

He grinned and pressed a finger into my slick hole. "Oh, I'm gonna fuck you, baby."

Torture, the best, most amazing, super, fucking outstanding torture. Atlas played my body, and every time I thought I'd come, he released me with a dark chuckle.

"You're evil." I was breathless as I watched Atlas stand, walk to the side table, and pull out lube and a condom.

"I'm a sin, remember?" Where he once said that with sadness, it was now said with acceptance. Not like he was okay with being a sin, but maybe seeing that not all pasts, no matter how dark, taint us forever or label us as something we don't feel we are.

"You can sin all over me." And then we were both bursting out with laughter over my corniness.

I opened my arms and Atlas fell into them, our bodies aligned, and we kissed. Quickly he slipped the condom on, rubbed lube over it, and in a flawless glide, was inside me.

"You always feel amazing," he said as he moved in long, deep thrusts.

"You always feel like you belong."

He pressed his lips to mine, tongue and teeth, and he moved faster, harder, driving us to orgasm. When we came together, mixing, loving, all the anxiety washed away. It was just us, and for the moment, we were okay.

———

MONDAY MORNING CAME with phones vibrating and people wanting to come up and talk to Atlas. Joker's Sin was allowed to open. The investigation did prove someone tampered with Ledger's controls, and inside the barrels of water there were traces of oleoresin capsicum, or as Atlas explained it, "The shit that's in pepper spray." All in all, Atlas was cleared of any wrongdoing, and while they were still investigating who could've done it, he was allowed to open.

There was no point in trying to tell the police it was Vick Keller; when we did, it was met with scorned responses and eye rolls. Atlas being able to have his club back was good news. By the afternoon, we were all down at the club, trying to see how we could reopen with pizazz.

"We need to do serious cleaning," Max said, and he was right.

While the police and fire department investigated, they didn't clean anything.

"We could maybe work up a cool Friday reopening. Build up the hype on the website and such. Tell the papers and news. Take the time to clean up and come up with a cool idea?" I said and when I was met with positive feedback, I was excited.

There was still no news from TJ about anything with Vick and Wang. When I texted Shane, he said things had been quiet. And that reminded me.

"Hey, Atlas." He was talking with Ledger about something but excused himself and came to me.

"What's up?"

"Okay, so if you say no, I'll understand. But, I have this friend, you see, right?"

He smirked. "Okay, just say it."

"He works at Vick's, he's like my best friend. Anytime anyone tries to leave Vick's, well, you know…he needs to get out of there, and the only place safe is here right now. Even if it's also a target." I had to chuckle at my logic.

"What's he do there?"

"He's a bartender. Really talented."

He took my face in his hands and kissed me. "Have him come in whenever we're here cleaning up. I'm sure we can find a place for him."

I leaped into Atlas's arms and kissed him until Max and the others were whooping and hollering.

I tried not to let the chaos and mayhem that was whipping all around us bother me. Maybe I was naïve or whatever, but it all seemed like it couldn't touch me. Oh, how I wished that was true.

When I called Shane that night to tell him the good news, while he was happy, I could hear something was wrong in his voice.

"What's going on, Shane?"

"Something weird. I was leaving work tonight, right? Vick was in his office with Liberio like always, door shut. I was punching out when there was a pounding on the back door."

All I could think was, at least I was talking with Shane so whatever it was, he was okay.

"Liberio came down the hall, grunted for me to get the fuck out, and opened the back door. There were three Chinese dudes there. If Liberio was worried it didn't show, but I had to wait until they got inside to get out of the place. When I did, I passed this big-ass limo, the window was cracked open, and holy fuck, Toby, it was Wang Zhao, the crime boss."

Oh, my God! "Are you sure?"

"Uh yeah, the guy is on the news a lot, and I see him at Vayne's sometimes when I pick up food. He has like, his own table there or something."

"Wow. Well, maybe Vick pissed him off, or maybe they work together." I couldn't let Shane know. If he knew, he'd be in danger.

"Great, that's all we need. A powerful crime boss in bed with Vick." He sighed loudly into the phone. "So, whatever. Can I come by the club tomorrow?"

"Yeah, sure. Atlas and I will be there about eleven."

"Great. See you then." He disconnected, and I went to where Atlas was reading something on his laptop in the living room.

"Atlas."

He lifted his head and quirked a brow.

"Shane will come by the club tomorrow at eleven, but he told me something."

I sat and told Atlas the entire story Shane told me. He was quiet as I went on and on. And when I finally finished, he rubbed his eyes.

"I'm gonna call Ciro. Sounds like whatever was going to happen is about to."

I left him to talk to Ciro and decided to take a shower and get comfortable. I hoped whatever shit rained down on Vick and Haven Hart missed me and everyone I cared about by miles.

CHAPTER THIRTY-NINE

Atlas

Ciro let me know he'd speak with TJ but that whatever Wang was up to, it was early days. We'd have to wait it out.

All morning Toby was talking up his friend Shane, telling me how amazing he was, funny, loyal, and how he would never have survived Vick's as long as he did without him. I knew the second Toby asked that I'd likely hire him. If he was the person Toby described, there was no doubt the others would like him too.

"I've hated leaving him there, but he was really good at keeping in touch, so I knew he was okay. I just hope he'll be safe after he leaves there." Toby's sympathy and worry were endearing, and all I wanted to do was reassure him.

"He will be, we'll make sure of it."

We had breakfast and made our way over to Joker's Sin. We were all sitting around a table discussing opening night ideas when there was a knock on the front door.

"Oh, that's Shane." Toby got up and went to go to the door, but Ciro stopped him.

"Do Shane's knuckles make a magical sound unique to your ears?" He was being sarcastic, but I got what Ciro was saying.

"No, that's stupid, Ciro."

"Then you don't know it's him. Have a seat, buttercup, I'll get it."

Toby rolled his eyes but did as asked. I leaned over and squeezed his hand. "We have to be safe."

"I know."

"Is this Shane?" Ciro asked, and we all turned. Toby got up, rushed over, and hugged him. "I'll take that as a yes."

"Yes, this is Shane. Shane this is Atlas, Ciro, who answered the door, Ledger, he's the DJ, and Max, he manages the bar section."

Shane was beautiful with bright-red hair, a small smattering of freckles, and piercing gray eyes. He was taller than Toby, but who wasn't? He had some muscle definition but not much.

"Hey, there." Max shook his hand. "If all goes well, you'll be working with me."

"Oh." Shane smiled, his pale skin pinking. "Awesome."

As he went around the table, Ledger was scoping Shane out, unsurprisingly. Max had too, but I also knew gingers weren't his type. When he got to me, I stood and shook his hand.

"Toby talks about you a lot, and if you're half as wonderful as he says you are, then I'm sure this'll just be a formality."

"Thank you for the opportunity, Mr. Durand."

"Atlas, please."

Talking with Shane felt easy. He was likable, funny, and I could see exactly why Toby was friends with him. There was no question—he was a perfect fit for our merry group. Max had plenty of bartenders, but they were all part-time, so taking time off wasn't easy for Max because he didn't have someone steady in it like he was.

"Shane, are you looking for full-time work?"

"Oh, yes. I need all the hours I can get." I wasn't going to pry, but there was a lilt of desperation in his tone.

"Great. Max runs the bar; he has many part-timers there, and I'm sure he'd love someone to be full-time to help him out so maybe he could take a night off."

Max's eyes widened in delight. "Oh shit, yeah. I'd love to teach someone some managerial duties, so in an emergency I could scream and there you'd be."

The table erupted in laughter, and I was glad to see Shane jump right in.

"Absolutely. At Vick's I run the bar and floor. It's small, but it's a lot of work. I totally understand."

We spoke for a little while longer about the jobs he handled, and then it morphed into stories about him and Toby. We stayed away from any horrible ones, and when we were all done, I had one last thing to talk to Shane about.

"We're all aware of the type of man Vick Keller is, Shane. If he finds out you even came here to interview, it'll be a nightmare for you. So, it's best you're not alone."

I could see worry on Shane's face; I'd seen it too many times on Toby's.

"I really appreciate it, but Vick doesn't know I came here today. I work tonight and should be fine. Once I start here, if I do, then I'll let you know."

I wanted to argue, but Shane was a grown man. "If you have any inkling that Vick knows you came here, text Toby, and someone will come pick you up."

"That's…" He dropped his gaze to his lap. "Thank you."

I met everyone's faces, and it was a silent agreement. "Shane, we open Friday. We'd love you to be here for that. We're in the planning stages, and if you can start tomorrow to help out, that would be great."

"What?" He beamed and laughed. "Seriously, just like that?"

"That's how it was with me too. But, Shane, the longer you're at Vick's, the worse it'll be. Start tomorrow and never look back. This place is amazing."

"Come here around noon tomorrow, I'll have paperwork ready for you. We can talk more then."

We said our good-byes, and Ciro said he'd walk Shane out.

"I think he'll be a great addition," Max said as he tapped the table with his hands excitedly. "Can't wait to get a night off."

"We've been closed for like, a week, you've had a ton of time off," Ledger said.

Max shot him the bird and said he had to go through the new inventory. We had so many great ideas for opening night.

"Good news," Ledger said. "Looks like none of those dancers are going to sue you for the acid shower."

"You heard from their lawyers?"

He shook his head. "Nah, heard from ours. Only you could fucking almost blind ten people, and they still love you." He chuckled and got up too. "I have to plan my music."

When we closed up for the night, Ciro hadn't heard any news from TJ. She said it was still quiet. So maybe when Shane saw Wang, it was a business meeting, and he hadn't clued in to Vick's deception.

We grabbed a pizza and returned to the penthouse.

"Opening night will be amazing," Toby said as we stepped into my place. Oddly, the lights didn't turn on.

"Did you shut the motion lights off?"

Toby shook his head. "I know you have when I've been here, because you don't want things going dark when I don't move for three seconds," he joked.

"Step back." I pulled Toby's arm and shut the door.

"What's wrong?"

I didn't answer right away; instead, I called George. "Hey, Mr. Durand, everything okay?"

"Has anyone been by to see me or any deliveries?"

"No, sir. Nothing during my shift. And you were leaving just as I was coming on."

"Okay, can you do me a favor and put a call into maintenance? I'd like them to check my lighting. My motion sensors aren't working."

"Sure thing, Mr. Durand. You have a nice evening."

"You too, George."

Opening the door once more, I flipped the light switch on. The setting was dim, and everything appeared to be okay.

"Atlas, you're paranoid, and you have every right to be. It's likely a glitch, or one of us forgot to set the sensor before we left." Toby took the pizza from my hand and moved toward the living room. "Now, come on, I'm starving."

CHAPTER FORTY

Toby

I could tell Atlas was having a hard time letting it go about the sensor lights, even after I told him they weren't on. His excuse was that someone could've turned them off. After pizza, I put on his favorite movie, but he was tense.

As I rested my head on his lap, I tried rubbing against his dick. He chuckled a few times, but when I peered up at him, his gaze was wandering over the place.

"It's really bothering you."

"Toby, I know it seems like I'm crazy, but with you here, with everything going on, I've been meticulous about security. I know I left the sensor on because I came back inside to do it."

I did remember Atlas saying he forgot something and going in to do it, but I never asked what. He wasn't ill; if he said he did it, then he did. The sudden thought that we weren't safe had me whispering into Atlas's ear.

"George said no one came in. Aren't there cameras all over this fancy place?"

He didn't wait until I moved to get up, so I practically fell off the couch as he ran toward his room.

"No, no, it's okay, I'm fine." I chuckled. When he re-entered the room, he had his laptop.

"You're a genius," he said opening his laptop.

"And for that compliment, you're forgiven for almost tossing me on the floor." Sitting on the arm of the large chair, I watched as Atlas logged into what appeared to be the building's security feed. "You can access this?"

"Everyone who lives in the building has access to corridor feeds and lobby ones. It's a huge perk." He clicked a few things, and the hallway outside his penthouse popped up.

I watched as we left this morning and Atlas went back in. I saw us get on the elevator, and then Atlas sped it up. We saw some security guys come up a few times walking the hallway, then leave.

The time read an hour before we came home, nothing yet. Just as I was about to say something, the elevator door opened on the screen. George appeared there. "Another round?"

"Maybe."

We watched as he crept by the door for a little too long, slid a card in the slot, popped the door open, and slid inside.

"What the fuck?" Atlas whispered.

A few seconds later he came out, but the door was left ajar. Then a couple of minutes after that a man came to the door.

"It's Liberio." I spoke softly. I'd know that man anywhere.

He was inside the apartment for about ten minutes and left, shutting the door behind him.

Seeing George on the screen answered the question of why George said no one was here.

Atlas put the laptop down and went over to the sensor panel. "Yeah, but what the fuck does the panel have to do with anything? It's weird." I would have thought George would be aware of the cameras everywhere. Clearly, George wasn't thinking, or he was forced to let Liberio in.

It was weird, I'd give him that. We knew Liberio had left, so he wasn't there. A short while after Liberio left, we had come home. But deactivating the sensor would make it obvious someone was here.

"Do you think he's just trying to scare you?" I asked, joining Atlas as he stared at the panel. We were both talking so softly, like we knew were being heard. And that thought made me realize we likely were.

"What if it has nothing to do with the lights, but like it's a switch. Knowing you'll go over to turn the light on. It would signal you're home so Vick knew."

Atlas whipped his head, facing me. "So it's bugged?" I was glad when he whispered. But there was also the creeping dread we were heard anyway.

Leaning into Atlas's ear, I said, "If the thing went poorly with Wang, and Vick was able to figure it out or even suspect it was us, he'd want to have proof to show Wang. So Wang could come after us and let him go. Vick's not dumb."

"This is ridiculous, Toby, water in the circuits." His expression belied his words. He was playing it up.

"Look, I'm just saying maybe that's why George came up here and the other person was a repair guy. You're paranoid," I fake-argued.

"Why didn't George say something?"

"He's human, Atlas, he likely forgot. We can ask in the morning."

"Fine." Atlas stepped back from the panel. "Let's go get ice cream. I need to get out of here."

"It's late."

"Then stay here, I'm going." I knew he wouldn't leave

without me, but if he was willing to leave me, Vick would be more convinced we thought we were safe.

"Fine, I'll come. I want some rocky road."

We grabbed our wallets and keys and left the penthouse. We opted not to use Atlas's car in case that was bugged now too. We called for an Uber and when we got in, he texted Ciro.

"He's gonna meet us at Two Scoops." It was a small ice cream parlor near Joker's Sin. At least I really would get ice cream out of this deal.

We had just sat down with our ice cream when Ciro and TJ walked in.

"So you think your place is bugged?" TJ asked.

"Yeah. And maybe my car." Atlas offered Ciro some ice cream.

"No, we're good. TJ has some news."

"Right. So, Wang certainly found out about the switch-up, but he's holding Vick responsible. I don't know how or why, but he gave Vick a deadline to either hand him the people who did it or get his supply back. Between you and me, I think he'll kill him anyway, but Vick is enough of a narcissist to think otherwise."

That made sense. "Yeah, it was all too much of a coincidence. Liberio probably set up the bugs and looked around real fast to see if he found any of the drugs."

"If what you're saying is true, then we just have to wait it out. I'm sure something will happen within the next twenty-four hours. Vick will have nothing, and Wang will want his head." Atlas was right.

"Yeah, but what, we go to your place and play chess or something? There's no way they didn't hear all the shit we said." I laughed.

"If you don't go home, he'll know something's up. Keep your conversations light. Maybe talk about how excited you are about the opening. If you don't return, it'll be worse. Talk about how worried you are and feed Vick's ego." TJ smiled. "He'll love that."

We finished our ice cream, and TJ promised to meet us at Joker's Sin the next day to see how the night went and if any more news surfaced. All I knew was that it was going to be a long night and a longer twenty-four hours. With the opening so close, Atlas didn't need all this stress. I only hoped Wang stepped in and dealt with Vick before Vick decided to take matters into his own hands.

When we walked into the penthouse, Atlas said out loud how happy he'd be when maintenance fixed the light.

"I do think you should talk to the property manager or whoever about George just entering people's homes, or at least not informing people that he would be going in for repairs." Even though I knew I'd spoken softly enough that it was Liberio in the video, we needed to show concern about strangers entering the penthouse.

"Check and see if anything was taken. Maybe the repair guy or George took something."

After we pretended to look things over, we took a shower, Atlas changed his alarm code because he was vigilant, and when we went into the bedroom he shut the door, locked it, and pushed the dresser in front of it.

"Love what you've done with the place," I whispered once he was in bed.

He pressed a kiss to my forehead. There was no way we were having sex, knowing Vick was listening.

"Night, babe."

"Night."

But we didn't sleep. We lay in silence, staring at the ceiling, knowing every breath we took, Vick was listening.

CHAPTER FORTY-ONE

Atlas

TJ came to Joker's Sin the following morning as promised. "On my way over, I saw a huge presence over at Vick's. Lots of fancy cars." She chuckled.

"Wang?" She nodded.

"We didn't say anything last night. Played it off convincingly, if I do say so myself." Toby was quite pleased with himself.

"Your opening is Friday?" TJ asked as she took the cup of coffee Toby offered.

"Yeah."

"So keeping things away from you is a good thing. Let Wang handle Vick for a while. Stay vigilant, remember the bugs, and let me know if anything weird, or weirder, happens. In return, I'll let you know if I hear anything." She took a few sips of her coffee and went to leave.

"Thanks for everything," Toby said.

"We're the good guys, we need to stick together." She passed Ciro on the way out, they spoke for a minute, then turned to leave when a loud blast shook the place.

"What the fuck!" Ciro shouted.

I grabbed Toby, pulling him to me and shielding him just in case there was another. I could feel him shaking, and his breathing was fast. When no other sounds were heard, I took his hand. "Stay with me." He nodded and we walked over to where Ciro and TJ stood.

"Everyone okay?"

"Yeah," she said. "It wasn't here; I've heard my fair share of explosions in my day. That was a little ways away."

I remembered last year when there was a huge explosion about ten blocks from here, an entire tower went down and rocked the whole city. But this one was closer, just not as powerful.

"Stay here." Ciro and TJ slipped outside. When they opened the door, smoke and dust filtered in. It was brief but whatever it was, it wasn't good.

"This fucking town," Max said as he came out of my office. He'd been printing the papers for Shane to sign later today. "I don't know why the fuck I stay here."

Everyone who lived in Haven Hart often had those thoughts. They'd always be quickly extinguished by an opposing thought of, *I wouldn't live anywhere else.*

Max, Toby, and I sat and waited for Ciro and TJ to return. Ledger wasn't coming in until later, and I knew he wasn't near here, so I didn't worry.

"I hope Shane is okay." Toby reached into his pocket for his cell phone, likely to check on him, when Ciro returned.

"TJ is staying on the scene and called for backup. Vick's place is destroyed. The whole left side is gone, and fire is taking the rest."

Holy fuck. "Could you see if Wang's cars were still there?"

He shook his head. "Too much smoke, but I don't think they were. Now to see if Vick or any of them were still in there."

"Shane said he heard the explosion but is fine. He was home, sleeping." Toby rested his head on my shoulder and sighed. "Maybe this is over now."

I really hoped so.

———

"THIS SALARY IS CRAZY GOOD, and the medical benefits are awesome." Shane was signing the paperwork, smiling in disbelief as he did.

"I don't think you'll be working at Vick's tonight, seeing as it's gone, so if you'd like to hang out and get a lay of the land with Max, go for it."

"Yeah. I can't believe someone blew the place up." He puffed out a mouthful of air. "Crazy shit."

"Could've been a gas line burst or something."

"Uh-huh, right. This is Vick. He probably has just as many enemies as he does boneheaded followers." Shane rose, hand out to shake. "Thanks, Atlas. I'd like to stay and talk with Max."

"Sure, and welcome aboard." I shook his hand and the second he left my office, Toby came in.

"I can't tell you how grateful I am that you hired Shane."

I opened my arms, and Toby fell right into them. I liked him like this, on my lap and in my arms. "He's a good fit, and you'll feel better that he's here and safe."

"Do you think Wang blew up Vick's place?" I felt his lips rubbing against my skin and damn, he was making me hard.

"Maybe, who knows? What I do know is, a world without Vick Keller is a better world." Toby's tongue slid over my skin, and I hummed. "Are you starting something?"

"I locked the door."

Turning my head, I took his mouth, loving how he sucked on my tongue. His taste was an addiction I didn't think I'd ever felt with anyone else.

"We don't have a lot of time, baby."

He broke the kiss, looking at me with lust-filled eyes. "I kinda want to be fucked on your desk."

Shit. "I'm all about fulfilling dreams." I scooped him up and placed him on my desk.

"I'm good with you just filling me."

Laughing, I quickly unbuttoned my pants and slid them down, Toby working on his own.

"That was so cheesy, and hot at the same time."

We laughed, kissed, and when I pulled Toby closer to the edge of my desk, I rubbed my hard shaft over his hole.

"Fuck me, Atlas. Just you, please?"

"I want that, so much. But not without being tested. We can do that together but for now…" I opened my desk drawer, pulled out a condom and lube. "I won't risk it."

His gaze went soft. "Okay, but you need to fuck me like, now."

I slipped the condom on, lubed up myself and my fingers. When I pushed one into him, he moaned beautifully, and I felt it all the way to my cock. By the time I had three fingers pumping into him, he was shaking and almost incoherent.

"Seriously, Atlas, please."

I removed my fingers, gripped my cock, and slid into his heat. "Damn, you feel like nothing I've ever felt. Each time."

After that it was moans, kisses, and skin on skin. Toby held his legs up and open. Hovering over him, I reached and cradled his head, slamming into him fast and hard. I longed to do this raw, feel my seed push into him, watch as it dripped out and shove it back in. To know I was in him long after I'd come.

"I'm coming," he said as he arched up. A second later, he came all over his stomach, a little on his shirt—but who the fuck cared? Fucking him through his orgasm, relishing how he clenched around me, it was all I needed, and then I was coming too.

We didn't bother dressing; I slid out, removed the condom, and carried him to my bathroom. We showered together with tender caresses and soft kisses. I was falling in love with Toby St. Claire, and it both terrified and exhilarated me.

When we were washed and dried, we redressed, glad that our clothes were salvageable. Sure, I had other clothes in my office, but if Toby had to walk out with wrinkled clothes, I would too.

The rest of the day was spent getting things ready for the reopening. As we all left that evening, we watched as fire trucks and police vehicles still surrounded Vick's place. TJ did say there was a dead body inside but no word yet as to who it was.

On our way home, we stopped at a diner for a quick bite. Honestly, we were just prolonging the inevitable of going back to my place, where we'd have to watch what we said. The property manager had contacted me after I informed him George came into my place uninvited, and promised he'd be dealt with. I knew George was likely threatened by Vick, and that was why I opted not to press charges, but I had to worry about Toby and our safety. The doorman told me today George was let go. It only made me feel marginally safer.

We entered the penthouse, sensor still not working, and watched TV. The news was talking about the explosion and claiming faulty wiring, but the investigation was ongoing. When we went to bed, I locked the door, pushed the dresser in front again, and with Toby cradled in my arms, fell into a fitful sleep.

CHAPTER FORTY-TWO

Toby

Atlas, Max, Ledger, Ciro, Shane, and I all stood on the stage of Joker's Sin. It was a couple of hours before opening night, and the rest of the staff hadn't arrived yet, but TJ had news. Ledger wanted to test the lighting anyway, so he asked for our help. TJ sat below us on a stool, and we all were on different areas of the stage.

"Sorry we have to talk like this," Atlas said. "We're running out of time."

"No, it's okay. I'm kind of enjoying this." She chuckled. "I just wanted to tell you the body from the explosion was identified as one Chester Romanski."

Forgetting about my position on the stage, I walked over to the edge, where TJ was reading off her tablet.

"That's impossible."

"I agree," Shane said standing beside me.

"I too found it odd since his body was found on the docks a few weeks ago." TJ sighed.

"Why would Vick do that?" Atlas asked.

"Funny thing about that. See, when Vick was questioned after that, he said Chester had an altercation here in Joker's Sin, and lo and behold, there was a police report on that. When we said his body was found on the docks a few weeks earlier, he said we were wrong. And when we went into the police records, guess what?"

"There was no record anymore," Ciro answered.

"Bingo!"

I remembered the fight outside the club, and I was sure Ciro and Atlas did too. "He got Chester's first murder erased and just moved the body to his place, blew it up, and is blaming Atlas for it?"

She nodded. "Yeah, it's totally unhinged. But he has the chief in his pocket, and God knows who else for now. I'm sure he didn't do all this shit on his own. My guess, Wang isn't waiting and Vick's nervous. He wants the insurance money, but he's vindictive and wants Atlas to pay for all of it too."

"He's getting ready to run?" Ledger laughed. "It will take a while to get the money from the insurance company. What's he gonna do in the meantime?"

"He's desperate," Ciro said. "That's worse than anything. He wants cops looking here, maybe he'll tell Wang his shit's here too. Then he runs."

"That's ridiculous. Wang wouldn't believe that." *Would he?*

"I paid a visit to Wang this morning," TJ said. That was very risky. "Not alone, don't panic. Wang is a cruel man. I wouldn't ask him to hold a ladder so I could climb up it. But he's also a proud man. He doesn't think for a second you're behind this, even though you are. He's out for Vick's blood. I told him I wouldn't stand in his way."

"So Vick wants to disappear, he's gonna hole up somewhere until his settlement, then run and because he's a psycho, he has to get one more punch into Atlas?" Max rolled his eyes. "Seriously, this fucking town!" he shouted, arms out in disbelief. "He's moving bodies, changing reports. How is this just being overlooked?"

"It's this town, Max. I like to think it won't always be this way. Just keep your eyes open, all of you. I think Wang will be ahead of him, and his plan won't even have a chance of blossoming. I'll hold the cops off. Don't worry." TJ bid us farewell and left.

"Let's concentrate on opening night," Atlas said, and while I wasn't as convinced as everyone else that Vick wasn't going to snap before he disappeared, I decided to busy myself with preparing for the doors to open.

———

THE OPENING WAS in full swing, and if anyone was nervous to come after the rain thing, it didn't show in the numbers. Shane was laughing and having an amazing time. I could see he and Max were working really well together. People were dancing, drinking, and it was like nothing ever happened.

"How you doing?" Atlas wrapped his arms around me from behind.

"Good. Everyone's having a blast."

"Thank fuck. I tell you, I was a little nervous."

Turning in his arms, I looked up into his honey eyes. "People like Vick make messes, but they never win in the end."

"Yeah. You know, I always knew the justice system in Haven Hart was fucked up. But seeing all this shit, how Vick just changes paperwork, and no one bats an eye. How drugs are everywhere, bodies line the street. How did it get so bad?"

I rested my head over his heart. "I think it's always been bad in a sense, but I also think because it's directly affecting you, now it feels magnified."

"Maybe. I dunno. It's crazy, though."

We were in agreement there. The whole thing felt unbelievable, like it was a Hollywood movie and we were thrown in the middle of it.

"Atlas!" Someone called his name, and he excused himself to talk to whoever it was.

For the rest of the night I checked on all the stations, made sure things were running smoothly, and let the sounds of Joker's Sin invade me.

When the doors closed for the night, everyone went into cleanup mode. Max, Shane, and the other four bartenders began their routine. Security started doing checks of the bathrooms, VIP area, parking lot. Everyone was busy. I was organizing things for tomorrow when I heard a crash and a curse.

"I'm sorry," Shane said.

"Nah it's okay." Max was wiping whatever spilled off his pants.

"What happened?" I asked.

"I was moving the three bottles of vodka and dropped one. I'm an idiot."

"You're fine." Max waved him away. "Let me go get another bottle."

"You go get cleaned up, I'll grab it. Which one is it?" Shane held up an unbroken one for me to see. "Okay, be right back."

Opening the door to the hallway that led to the storage room, I was hit with a rush of cold. The door was ajar—probably security out walking the parking lot. *The idiots have keys.* I'd have to talk to Atlas about that; it was dangerous.

The storage area was huge, filled with so many bottles, cans, and kegs. But, Max was meticulous about his booze, and I knew he alphabetized it all. So Vodka was under V and the brand was in alphabetical order under V. A library of liquor. I chuckled as I moved toward the V shelf.

I found the bottle and was making my way toward the exit

when I heard a slam. I walked faster and saw that the storage door had shut.

"Oh, please don't be locked." I got to the door, and sure enough, it was locked. Placing the bottle down, I reached for my cell phone. I'd text Atlas to let me out. Probably the fucking wind because the back door was left open.

I just started texting when the door opened.

"Oh, thank…" My words froze when I saw Liberio standing there and when I backed up, I hit something, or someone.

"Well, hey there, Toby. Long time no see." Vick cackled in my ear.

I was about to scream, but he wrapped his hand around my mouth. I kicked but only knocked the bottle down.

"Help me, Liberio," Vick said and Liberio picked up the bottle and hit me over the head. Then there was nothing.

CHAPTER FORTY-THREE

Atlas

"What did you do?" I came out of the office to see Max wiping his crotch.

"Shane slipped and dropped the vodka, no big. Toby went to get another, and Shane's grabbing the dustpan and broom."

"Okay."

"Maybe check on Toby, he's been back there for like, ten minutes. I organized that storage room for quick in and out."

"Sure," I said.

I went down the hallway and noticed the storage door was shut. Toby probably locked himself in. Chuckling, I opened the door and stopped cold. Glass and moisture were all over the floor.

"Toby?" There was no answer so I carefully crept inside, pulling my cell phone out at the same time. I hit the button for Ciro.

"Yeah."

"Storage room, now." I disconnected.

I searched the entire room, and there was no sign of Toby. By the time Ciro got there, I knew he wasn't here.

"Something happened," I said to Ciro as he looked at the glass on the ground.

"I'll call TJ." He stepped out and I started checking the closets, anywhere he may be hiding or God forbid, stuffed. Each passing second we couldn't find him, an echoing throb of despair threatened to cripple me.

"He has him!" Shane yelled as he came running from outside. He was shaking a piece of paper. "I went outside to dump the glass in the bins since we'd already tossed the garbage. This was taped to your car. I thought it was a ticket and was gonna bring it in for you but, here, look." He thrust it at me, and I opened it.

Maybe the games are fun after all.

"Where would he take him?" I asked as I crumpled the paper in my fist.

"His building is condemned; I can go check, though," Ciro offered. "TJ's on her way."

"Wang?" Ledger's voice cracked when he said it. Thinking that Toby was with Wang Zhao and Vick Keller was an unthinkable thing.

"Where would Wang be?" Shane's face pinked, his bottom lip trembled. "He's been through so much already. Why can't Vick leave him the fuck alone?"

"Hey." Ledger spun Shane around, so they were facing each other. "We take care of our own. We'll find him." When Shane lunged into Ledger's arms and sobbed, there was no hiding the shock on his face, but he hugged Shane back and let him cry.

"Ciro, check out Vick's. Where's Wang known to go?" I asked anyone who'd know.

"He owns a large area, Atlas." Max pulled out his phone. "This place though, wasn't it on the news like a month ago when they talked about a huge mob presence with the Zhao family?"

Paradise Pavilion was a high-class restaurant specializing in traditional Chinese cuisine. I'd gone there once for a dinner meeting and knew where it was.

"Right. You think he's there?"

Max shrugged. "If he's not, whoever's there would be able to get a message to him. Even if Toby isn't there, I'm sure Wang wants to find Vick."

It was a good thought.

"Okay, I called in all my eyes and ears in the city," TJ said as she entered the club. "I agree Paradise Pavilion is a good place to start."

Ciro returned shaking his head. "No one's at Vick's."

Pulling my keys from my pocket, I started toward the door. "Whoever's coming, let's move."

No one stayed behind.

EVEN THOUGH IT was way past business hours, when my car and Ciro's pulled up to the restaurant, two men met us at the door.

"Mr. Zhao has been expecting you, Mr. Durand," one of the men said. I thought for sure they'd frisk us, but they never did, just opened the door for us to enter.

I didn't say anything, unwilling to accidentally offend or regret my words. I followed one of the men, aware the other was flanking our large group. He brought us all the way to the back, where there was a large table filled with food.

The red and gold walls that were adorned with drawings of birds I didn't recognize gave the place a unique elegance. The man who sat at the head of the table, however, was the epitome of lethal.

"Mr. Durand," Wang said as he sat comfortably in his chair. His dark hair was slicked back, and eyes the color of obsidian glared at me. His shirt was blood red and the only color his attire had. On either side of him were four men and two more behind him. I had no doubt if I turned around, my entire group would be surrounded.

"Mr. Zhao, I apologize for interrupting you at this late hour. But I'm hoping you could be of some assistance."

He smirked, but it wasn't cute or endearing. It was terrifying. "You lost something, I assume." Wang gestured to one of his men. "Jin, please bring in our guests."

"Toby's here?" I asked taking a step forward, only to be stopped with a hand on my shoulder.

"It would be wise you stay where you are until the conclusion of our meeting." Wang quirked a brow.

The double doors to the kitchen opened. Toby, with his hands tied and mouth gagged, was being led out by Wang's man, Jin. Behind him, not tied or gagged, were Vick and Liberio. If they weren't tied up, this couldn't be good. In my mind, I kept seeing Joker the day he died. Me on the other side of the room, help-less...useless. I couldn't be those things for Toby.

"Mr. Durand, do you know my business associate, Mr. Keller?"

"Unfortunately."

Wang laughed. "Yes, he is a bother sometimes, we can agree."

Vick glared at Wang for the briefest of moments—no question, he didn't want to get on Wang's bad side.

"Mr. Keller has spun me quite the tale. He says you meddled in my affairs and because of that, I'm out over five million dollars and a lot of cocaine. Tell me, Mr. Durand, is this true?"

I was glad my friends weren't speaking or moving. They were a silent support, and I knew if I fucked this up, they would pay for my mistakes.

"Mr. Zhao. As you know, I've run a club for many years here in Haven Hart. I cause no trouble and don't seek it out. Mr. Keller, on the other hand, has repeatedly tried to dismantle my business and if I was a betting man, I'd put money on the fact that he's trying to set me up, so you'll get rid of me."

Wang nodded. "I do agree Mr. Keller would be very happy if I rid you from this earth."

Toby was struggling, trying to speak. I shook my head at him. "He blew up his own business to get the insurance money and run. If he was so innocent, why'd he feel the need to run?" I'd be fucked if Wang asked me for any proof, so I had to hope I sounded convincing.

Wang's eyes widened and his glare turned to Vick. "So, not gas or electrical, then?"

"Don't listen to him, Zhao, he's trying to save his own ass." Vick's face was red with rage.

"Except he's telling the truth," Tracey spoke up. "Mr. Zhao, we've spoken, I told you I'd stay out of your way when dealing with Mr. Keller. However, I can't ignore it if you harm Atlas, Toby, or any of these people here. They're innocent. Vick here's gotten himself into a bad situation and is doing what snakes do and trying to slither away."

"Yes, Detective Wilding, a pleasure to see you again."

It was quiet for a few minutes while Wang stared down at his tea. I wished I could tumble around in his head and know what he was thinking.

"Okay, then. It's quite clear what needs to happen here." He looked up, right into my eyes, his expression placid.

"There's one man who's gotten too big for this city. One man above all others that needs to go. I'm sorry, Mr. Durand."

I barely had time to process what he was saying when a single shot was fired.

CHAPTER FORTY-FOUR

Toby

The spray of blood spattered across my face, and instinctively I jerked away. A loud crash made me yelp, and the man who was holding me pulled me away from the falling body.

Liberio. I stared as a pool of crimson spread around his head…his head with a rather large bullet wound through it.

"What the hell!" Vick shouted.

"What the hell indeed, Mr. Keller. This wall, that is now nothing but a bag of bones, was your biggest and best defense. A threat to me, and judging by what I've heard, quite the tormentor of anyone who wronged you." Wang's entire attention was on Vick, and I watched Atlas as he stared at me. Fear, worry, and longing shone in his honey eyes, and I wanted to leap over the table and jump into his arms. Arms I always felt safe in.

"What about him?" Vick pointed to Atlas. "He has five other people with him. How is that not threatening?"

Wang stood and was in front of Vick so fast, hand around his neck before I even realized he'd moved.

"How dare you speak to me in such a manner, Mr. Keller. I will not tolerate it. You've done well by me for many years, but the first sign of deceit and you turn into a whimpering, spiteful man. It's unbecoming."

My only hope was that Wang would kill Vick and let us all go. Being so far from the others, I couldn't help but think I would meet the same fate as Liberio. And with that horrible thought, I closed my eyes and focused on good things. Poppy's laugh, the feel of Atlas's lips, hands, and skin, the smell of coffee in the early morning outside Quirks and Perks, the vibration music makes through my body when I'm at Joker's Sin, all the themed nights at the club, Shane's horrible jokes. Over and over again I replayed those memories. If I was going to die here today, I'd die not seeing it coming but instead being lost in my happiness.

"Mr. St. Claire?" The sound of Wang's voice so close to me forced me to squeeze my eyes tighter.

"Toby," Atlas said louder and instinctively I opened my eyes, but it wasn't Atlas in front of me, it was Wang.

"Why are you closing your eyes?" Wang removed the gag so I could answer.

"I wanted to die remembering the things I loved."

Judging by his expression, the answer must've surprised him. "And what do you love, Mr. St. Claire?"

Such an invasive question but what did it matter at this point? "My sister, my friends…" My throat began to clog, and I felt the tears run down my cheeks. "Coffee, music." I couldn't stop the way my voice cracked or the sob that broke free. "Atlas. I love him so much."

"I see." Wang didn't appear to be phased by my falling apart or anything, really. He peered over his shoulder. I followed his line of sight to where Atlas stood, stoic, but there was no missing the redness in his eyes.

"You love Mr. St. Claire, Mr. Durand?"

"I do." He didn't hesitate, and that just made me cry harder.

"This is motherfucking bullshit. What does two fags loving each other have to do with anything?" Vick shouted, and with a nod of Wang's head, Vick was flying through the air and slammed against the table covered with food.

"I've had quite enough of your disrespect, Mr. Keller. You came into my place of business, told me you had brought me the man who helped steal my drugs and my money. What I see before me is a man, Atlas Durand, who is wealthy in his own practices and has never dipped into the pools you have." Wang turned to me. "Then Toby St. Claire who, and take no offense, Mr. St. Claire, wouldn't harm a fly or risk getting a parking ticket. Then we have you."

Wang's man lifted Vick off the table, food and porcelain scattered to the floor, and I took a step back.

"In the last month alone, you abused your own worker, you tried to damage Mr. Durand's business countless times, blew up your own business for insurance money, and stole my drugs."

"Mr. Zhao, I swear I didn't…"

"Silence!" Wang shouted and damn, the man had a loud voice. "Your actions tell a story, Mr. Keller, and the fact that you were going to run while Mr. Durand just had a reopening is very illuminating. Don't you think, Jin?" He turned to a man a few feet from him.

"I do, sir."

"Mr. Keller, I regret to inform you, I no longer require your business. Your existence is bothersome, and you're causing ripples where none are wanted. Jin here will escort you out. Good night."

What? He was just going to let him leave? That would never stop Vick; he'd come right back.

"Please, Mr. Zhao, I swear I didn't do this, I'm innocent."

Wang chuckled darkly. "You are far from innocent, Mr.

Keller." With a curt nod to one of his men, Vick was dragged out, kicking and very loudly screaming.

I wanted to ask if Wang was serious, if he was really going to just let Vick go. He had to know Vick wasn't a man to be trusted. But Wang spoke before I could.

"Mr. Keller will no longer be an issue for either of us. He will no longer be an issue for anyone ever again; I'm sure you understand my meaning." I watched as he moved closer to Atlas, and fear prickled up my spine. "I've never had issue with you, Mr. Durand. As a matter of fact, your club brings many people to Haven Hart. That's very good for my business."

If looks could incinerate, Atlas's glare would set him ablaze.

"You don't approve." Wang chuckled. "I do not care if you do or don't. But I have no issue with you or your lover here." He gestured to me, and then the binds tying my hands together were severed.

"However, I do not wish to cross paths again. I'm not sure what exactly happened to my drugs, and I may be a fool to think you are innocent in the situation, but I will give you this pass. Do you accept it?"

Atlas's nostrils flared, and I knew he wanted to punch Wang but instead he calmly said, "I do."

"Very good. You may all go. Have a good night."

With that, Wang walked around Atlas and our friends and left the restaurant. One of Wang's men dragged Liberio's body through the kitchen—*Mental note, never eat here*—and another guy gave me a nudge, telling me to move. Not having to be told twice, I ran to Atlas, and when I got there, he gathered me in a fierce hug, his lips slammed into mine, and whispers of I love you were said between kisses.

"Take me home, Atlas."

"I'll take you anywhere, Toby."

EPILOGUE

Six Months Later
Atlas

"I don't understand, why did they have their bachelor party so far from their wedding date?" Toby asked as we sat in the middle of a lavish garden, in mid-October, watching the senator's son Sam and his fiancé, Jeremy, exchanging vows.

"I think it had something to do with spreading it out. I don't know and don't care. I'm more shocked they invited us." And I was. After the shit show that happened with my club and them not really knowing me well, to get an invite to their wedding was amazing.

I was going to decline, but between Toby and Poppy, they wouldn't let me. And so I only agreed as long as Toby attended as my plus-one.

"It's so gorgeous. I can smell autumn in the air, the colors are stunning, and they're lucky it's not raining."

They were being married outside Haven Hart only for security reasons, the senator had said. But there was a lot going on in

Haven Hart, and it wasn't so safe—something the senator might want to fix before re-election.

"I do." Jeremy beamed at Sam, and when the officiant pronounced them married, their kiss was adorable. Sam dipped Jeremy, and the crowd cheered.

"That was lovely." Toby wiped a tear and I smiled. I loved this man more every single day.

For the last six months, he'd been by my side with the club, making it even better than it already was. When I said I had a problem staying in my penthouse after the break-in, even after Ciro went in and removed every bug and fixed my sensors, he helped me find a new place. One I asked him to move into with me. With Desi and Poppy living together in a house outside the city, it was silly to have him all alone in that shitty apartment. So, when he said yes, I was thrilled.

Wang was right when he said Vick would no longer be a problem for us. A couple of months later, a very decomposed body was found in a shipping crate. TJ later told us it matched Vick's DNA. It had been quiet—well, as quiet as anything could be, and I'd loved every second.

We were sitting together, finishing our meal, when the song that started it all began to play. That night, when I took Toby in my arms in front of everyone at Joker's Sin and danced with him, was the beginning of something I didn't even know would be anything.

Toby looked at me with smiling eyes and held out his hand. "They're playing our song."

"They sure are."

We made our way to the dance floor, and like that night, I lifted him in my arms and danced with him. I didn't think I'd ever felt love like I did when I was with Toby, but here in my arms was everything…my everything.

When the song ended we turned, and Sam and Jeremy stood there with matching smiles.

"You two are gorgeous together," Sam said. "I don't believe we had the chance to meet. I'm Sam Ramos, and this is my husband, Jeremy Ramos." They both chuckled at the introduction.

"It's wonderful to meet you. Thank you for inviting us, this is…wow," Toby said.

"Joker's Sin is important to Haven Hart. It's the beat to the heart." He winked at his own pun. "We need more safe places like it. I admire Atlas a great deal."

I was rendered speechless at Sam's words. "Thank you, Sam, that means a lot to me."

"Well, we need to make rounds, thanks for coming."

Toby was hysterically laughing after they walked away. "That is so cool! You're famous. Well, sort of."

Pulling Toby into another dance I said, "I don't need fame, I just need you."

"Totally cheesy." He laughed.

"I'm fine with that."

For the rest of the night we danced, in sync in every way. Because of this amazing man in my arms, I didn't feel like Joker's sin anymore. Toby made me feel virtuous; he took away my guilt and replaced it with love, forgiveness, and purpose.

"Thank you, Toby," I whispered to him.

"For what?"

"Everything."

Author's Note

WANT to go on a date with Atlas and Toby? There's a free short story in my reader group: https://www.facebook.com/groups/DavidsonKingsCourt/

There are giveaways, exclusive material, teaser, and so much more. Hope to see you there.

Also, keep up with my new releases and info on book, translations, audios, and more by joining my newsletter: https://www.davidsonking.com/subscribe

Thank you so much for reading Atlas and Toby's story. Feel free to leave a review. I'd love to know what you thought.

OTHER BOOKS BY DAVIDSON KING

HAVEN HART SERIES:

Snow Falling

Hug It Out

A Dangerous Dance

Snow Storm

From These Ashes

Triple Threat

Raven's Hart

Collaboration with JM Dabney

The Hunt

Standalones

New Tricks (Book 10: Ace's Wild multi-author series)

Sticky Fingers

ACKNOWLEDGMENTS

There are so many people to thank I fear I will always forget someone. Of course my family. They have to put up with my crazy brain on a regular basis. I also want to thank my Beta Team: Jenn, Luna, Annabella, Morningstar, Lori, and Steph. They get my books in their rawest forms and lovingly rip it to shreds. I couldn't do it without them. I want to thank Anita for her special catches. She's more a magician than anything else. Thank you to Alice for being so great soundboard and idea girl, she's awesome. Flat Earth Editing, Hope and Jess, made this book sparkle in the end and it has been a pleasure working with them. And of course I have to thank Designs by Morningstar for the cover. She brought Atlas to life on this cover brilliantly.

In the end none of this happens without all of you reading my insane ideas. This is for you, my readers. You amaze me and inspire me every day. Thank you, a million times.

ABOUT THE AUTHOR

Davidson King, always had a hope that someday her daydreams would become real-life stories. As a child, you would often find her in her own world, thinking up the most insane situations. It may have taken her awhile, but she made her dream come true with her first published work, Snow Falling.

When she's not writing you can find her blogging away on Diverse Reader, her review and promotional site. She managed to wrangle herself a husband who matched her crazy and they hatched three wonderful children.

If you were to ask her what gave her the courage to finally publish, she'd tell you it was her amazing family and friends. Support is vital in all things and when you're afraid of your dreams, it will be your cheering section that will lift you up.

Check out my Linktree for all links: https://linktr.ee/davidsonkingauthor

www.ingramcontent.com/pod-product-compliance
Lightning Source LLC
Chambersburg PA
CBHW050506160726
48003CB00001B/190